PANDEMIA

Wading Through The Pandemic

Serene T. Marshall

First paperback edition June 2023

Cover design by Kamar Martin

ISBN: 9798987941713 Paperback
ISBN 9798987941720 ebook
ISBN 9798987941706 Hardcover

ACKNOWLEDGEMENTS

Thank you to the Legacy Leavers team, Makini Smith, and editor, Ann Marie Collymore, for patiently guiding me through this lengthy project and the edits. Thank you to Eva Myrick, MSCP of Simply Affirm, LLC, for your timely assistance. Thank you to Kamar Martin for the creative visual portrayal of this work. Alexia at Bookishends, thank you for being a willing and timely beta reader. Thank you to my brother Trevor for reading this work and for your input, support and encouragement during the process. Thank you to my family, including those ancestors who came before me, the ones whom I have not met, whose tenacity and grit paved the way and provided opportunities for me to pursue my dreams. May this work inspire those who dared to dream and may have been delayed or have changed lanes along the way. Finally, for my friends who offered kind words of encouragement, I thank you.

CHAPTER 1

Uncle B pointed the remote towards the screen against the wall, clicking hastily to crank up the volume as he always did, drowning out the pulsating soca music from the adjoining room. The adults made their way to the large couch in the far corner of the living room, waiting for the latest update on the impending pandemic.

"One hundred twenty-two new cases reported today, over two-thirds in the tri-state area alone. Passengers from several countries will not be allowed in as of today. All international flights entering the country will be monitored as a precaution, and testing is now mandatory. This mandate will be extended indefinitely. Stay tuned; we will keep you updated with more breaking news."

"Lawd, it's spreading fast," he muttered.

Having their music snuffed out by the evening news anchor, the children filed slowly into the den and plopped down on the rug in front of their elders. Each one stared blankly at the screen, unaware of the severity that lay ahead.

"Make this stop, now…now," Deron whispered and pointed at the screen, shaking his index finger, his eyes half-closed.

"Shhh," his little sister begged, sporting a heavy scowl.

"Just wanted to rescue us from the news," he replied, pointing again, the other hand circling above her head before diving down into her thick braids.

Aunty Mel looked over, eyes squinting beyond her square glasses. Her expression was enough to dispense silence for another fifteen minutes. They turned quietly to the news in progress.

"The public is advised to follow cautionary social distancing procedures newly implemented. Wash your hands, wear a mask or face covering, stand a few feet away from others whenever possible, avoid crowded areas and report any symptoms to your physicians."

"Mask, what masks? It's not carnival time yet," Uncle B chuckled, conversing with the screen.

His wife sighed, avoided eye contact and nervously bit her bottom lip, her stomach in knots. His broad shoulders and off-beat sense of humor drew her in years ago, but she plum forgot about that on days like today.

"Just in, I repeat, the travel ban has been extended indefinitely, including cruise ship passengers. We have Dr. Alexander Orci from the CDC to bring us an update on this virus."

"Man, they're restricting flights out now," groaned Uncle B. "Don't know if we're gonna get out of here in three days. Not sounding good at all. Slim chance."

"And, those poor people stuck on them ships out there, for how long?" his wife muttered. He removed his cap to reveal a head of thick salt and pepper hair and sunk further into the couch. B looked at the children and pointed to the den, the universal sign of freedom. They leapt up from the rug and headed across the room, far away from the somber talking heads. They were anxious to finish their new and improved dance routine to the newly released song they had on loop for the past hour. Viruses were not a part of their routine at this moment, and death was the farthest from their thoughts. The choreography was finalized earlier that week over protests and popcorn. As

for this news, the grownups were left to swallow that pill. And
so they began;

> *Hands to the left, right foot forward,*
> *Hands to the right, left foot forward,*
> *Pause,*
> *point left, point right*
> *Turn around, around, sing the chorus,*
> *whine up, whine up.*

CHAPTER 2

"When my mother first came to this country, things were much less complicated, but in some ways, much the same," I reminded the group again.

"I know what you mean. They start rounding up immigrants again, just like they did when they raided the subways in the early seventies," Trina echoed over the crowded table of Ruby's Caribbean Restaurant. They gathered weekly for girls' night out as time permitted, but with the country's current state, there was little time for get-togethers.

She took another generous sip of her red cocktail, swallowed with a nod of approval, and lifted her glass in my direction, "Tania, let's hear it," a signal to begin the discussion.

This was my night to tell my mother's story, as immigration was now a lightning rod issue that would be front and center on voting day. I could not join the group often since my school and new babysitting schedule did not allow it. Now that she was no longer with us, I was grateful to tell her story, which she said happened decades ago and was as relevant today as it was then.

"My mother said when she first came to this city in the seventies, police would come into the subways unannounced, 'doing raids' she called it—walking from one train car to another, demanding 'working papers,' searching all cars for illegal immigrants. Sometimes the officers would enter from the middle of the train, spanning out on both sides; other times, they would start from one end, moving from car to car, demanding proof of status."

"Ma said she had to always walk with her working papers, the ones that were renewable every five years and allowed her to work with a family as a nanny. It was a scary time, she said. Once, she told me she almost got caught without them; if you got caught, they did not always give you time to get them. On one occasion, she missed a raid by one train ahead, and not carrying her papers could have gotten her deported. Until her citizenship was finalized, it was precarious. Rest her soul. My mother would not want to see how things have evolved today. I am reminded of the comment she would sometimes make. *"Dey say dat tings change, but gyal, lemme tell you, dey stay the same."* Procedures are much more complicated now than when she came in, and as we all can see, the disdain for immigrants, Black and Brown, is a dire mess. The plight and struggles of some people have been blatantly ignored and made trivial while the same problems for other groups are given empathy and a sure way into this country. It's clear that the rules are not universal when it comes to immigration."

"Well, that's where we're headed again. Every vote counts," Lee stressed, the youngest and most vocal of the group. Just last month, she gave a presentation to her class on the state of immigration today. "We have to get more of the older heads registered to vote, and many of them in the district are hard to convince," she continued, pulling her cascading braids away from her face, smiling at the nods of approval from the group.

"I know." Trina seconded. "Here are the main reasons given from the last poll we took. Some people are very private, others fear government involvement, some are not involved in politics, others are heading back home to retire, and some just can't be bothered." Trina counted off the reasons, pointing to the survey results on her screen with blue manicured fingers as she continued. "And a select few argued that we are all puppets being bounced around by both parties. Those are just some of the excuses I get when canvassing."

"How're my sizzlin' hot ladies doin' tonite?" Will, the owner, stopped to check on his table of regulars. "My Sisters on the Pulse." he jokingly call us. And the name stuck. That's how we are known in the community.

"Rum and passion fruit? Or passion fruit and rum for my special table? A pitcher coming right up," he announced and headed to another table nearby. He treated them well, knew their favorite treats and was generous with offers. They were always present at this large corner table with their tablets and flyers, ruminating over the latest community project. And, as always, he knew exactly what they wanted without asking.

"We need all the pitchers we can get over here," Jemma shouted, shaking her empty glass in his direction, causing the remaining ice cubes to knock against the side of her glass. He turned sporting a mock frown in her direction.

"Well, I know that," he chuckled, darting under the palm trees lining the bright yellow corridor as he headed toward the bar. Without a glance at the offerings, we already knew what we would be ordering. The menu was scrumptious and season-al. Some dishes offered were only available at certain times of the year, and we all looked forward to it. Rice and peas, with stewed chicken, was a daily staple. There was coco bread, salt fish, souse, pig feet, and if we were lucky, his famous cow heel soup on Wednesdays. On some weekends, patrons could enjoy his barbeque specialties, escovitch fish, and, if you were overly picky, a savory jerk with a choice of two types of meat.

"I wish they could get some Oil Down in here," Jean mused.

"If you can get our breadfruit in bulk," Trina pointed at her laughing, he'll make it happen. Take a flight down tomorrow morning, make it happen, never mind the travel ban. Girl, you can make it happen."

"You know," Melva interjected, bringing the meeting back into focus, "the sad thing is there was another report of a child dying in the migrant detention center last Tuesday. Then another boat capsized last weekend with over seventy of our people, many died before rescue came. Ungodly. And don't forget poor people stranded for days under that bridge with not even the most basic of necessities."

Mya looked tired and leaned into the group. "Do you believe this is the U.S. we're talking about? In this century?" She leaned in with her usual hushed tone as though it was the most explosive report of the day.

"Yes, land of the free for some, when it's convenient, and what do you think about the election meddling?" she continued.

"What goes around comes around. The U.S. has been meddling in other countries' affairs for eons, backing and supporting one crook against another for its own interests. Now, it's back at you," she said, her voice rising. "Not surprising when karma hits back."

"True, so true." Melva agreed, nodding incessantly. "Problem is the entire country suffers for it."

To everyone's delight, Will reappeared carrying a tray filled with goodies, stopping to deliver an extra large pitcher of the house special for them.

"Passion fruit for my ladies!" He did not wait for Trina to answer. It was her favorite drink, so he topped her up first without question. He then filled all the glasses, depositing the half-empty pitcher in the center of the long table for their second round. The tray perched on his shoulder descended to reveal scrumptious coconut appetizers which he deposited next to the pitcher for us to enjoy while we continued our discussion.

"Well, since I missed your birthday celebration last week, here's to you," he pointed to Jean, all smiles.

"Thank you, dear. So thoughtful, isn't he?" Jean chuckled. Melva had already reached for a warm sample before the birthday girl had a chance to as we surveyed the platter filled with mouthwatering delights.

"Well, like the old folks say, one day at a time, little by little." She grabbed a coconut sugar cake, the scent wafting up from the large dish.

With the elections just a few months away, we could not meet as often as before, using the precious time we had together to organize voters in the community. That night, after discussing the presentation in more detail, we revamped the agenda and enjoyed the evening, a welcomed respite from our tight schedules. It would be a long while before I could meet with them again, our schedule was changing drastically. Just at the same time everything else was changing.

"We'll start with the Southbend neighborhood, agreed?" I questioned, awaiting a reply from Jean.

"That would be best. We could wrap up there in a week," she nodded.

The plan was in motion to start early next week, from the middle school heading south and across the six-lane divided highway.

"You know, there are quite a few retirees in that area. I remember it well. Some of the older heads who are not citizens try to avoid politics. There are rumors swirling about losing their green card and having benefits cut."

The birthday girl groaned, taking another sip from her bright green glass, as she not so quietly removed her heels underneath the table. The drink began peeling off her worries causing her shoulders to relax. The rest of the table would soon catch up.

"Not true at all. These silly stories." Trina peered into her tablet, color-coded by area. "I'll start in this section. You can pick your area." Everyone pointed to the screen and picked a color by location in proximity to our homes.

"I'll send the email tonight with more details. We have to print the flyers. They're mostly seniors. Social media will not work as well in this area."

Will checked in to see if we needed anything else. Jean lifted her glass, offering up a slow turn of her head and plastered a sad look at the dwindling pitcher.

The table was cleared, and we relaxed, welcoming the end of a long day. The evening was perfect, topped off by the arrival of hot food. It was mouth-watering as always and, at that moment, all-encompassing.

BLOG I

Another day, another injustice. Nothing new. A young lady in her twenties, full of promise, was shot by the police at night in her own home. As always expected, they will get off with no accountability. She was Black, like me. Who is gonna even bother to do the right thing for us in the 'greatest democracy on earth?' They would use the age old, generational, rigged-up judicial system to avoid any responsibility to justify murder every time.

And don't leave out the double-minded evangelicals, who say that we are equal, but cannot accept that we, too, are created in the image and likeness of God. Just like these chess-playing officials – the crooked voting laws, gerrymandering, and asinine voter ID games created by these states for the sake of rigging votes. How about the entire penal system, subpar loans, housing and food deserts—yes that's what they're called now, air and water pollution of entire communities? How much more can one of the richest countries on earth dish out to some of its citizens and expect to continue prospering for the next hundred years? Unscathed? Really?

This country continues to heap perils on its head, built without a proper foundation, at some point, will not stand. It will come crashing down. History has reflected this so many times. It's what will happen unless we fix the problem. Now, there is so much smoke smoldering right here in this collective kitchen, and so many people keep walking around with blinders.

You don't want to acknowledge a part of your family that you ignore and don't want to claim them because you think you are certified and legitimate. They are not and can't possibly be accepted as equals. And because you really don't ever want to share the Creator's bounty with anyone else, you really believe the entire planet belongs to only you. When you need them to help with the fire, it may be too late, and you may just reap what was sowed.

And by the way, this fuss about arms, you can arm yourself all right, but know that you are not the only one with arms. Arming yourself may give you a false sense of security and bolster your false sense of superiority and privilege. Remember, others are armed too. South of the border has millions of arms. Many of their stashes went over the border from, guess where- this country. Arms and nukes are everywhere, and there will be no other house for you to go back to when the bullets are coming back at you. Funny thing is, we don't know who or from what directions the consequences will come and how long they will last. Maybe another virus, who knows. The burning house that you ignited will be the only house. Remember that. And praying when you didn't take the time or courage to do the right thing when you had the time and opportunity, well, that won't work either. God says he will laugh at your calamity.

CHAPTER 3

Melva came in from the shopping outlet downtown, the one with the large, three-storied bargain department store where you could rummage for hours. You can find everything from BVDs for men, ladies underwear and lingerie to scuba equipment, pots, and pans. Determined to pack the suitcases, just in case they could find a flight, she had to buy a last-minute list of items for family members on the island. The list was for various products that were too expensive or too scarce to find on the island.

Yesterday at the pharmacy, she bought the hearing aid batteries and a donut cushion for Cousin Lester, and the chocolate protein drink, for an elderly relative refusing to eat solid food as of late. *"Not the white powder, is the real chocolate I drinkin,"* was the blunt request.

This trip was up in the air. The last items of clothing and household goods were finally collected, and she stood in the driveway deliberately pulling bags from the trunk. Finally, she climbed the stairs and rang the bell.

Uncle B opened the door and looked down at her feet. He smiled and counted out loud a grand total of eight shopping bags as he shook his head and offered to help. Some were heavy.

"What you have in this bag here? A toilet?"

"There is no flight out woman, none. You gon' have to return half of these knick-knacks in a few weeks, bet you."

There were no definite dates, no clear schedules, and no dining out anymore, but Melva was determined to maintain some level of normalcy. She did not want to argue. Let B quarrel if he wanted to. She continued her routine as she knew it.

After supper, she packed the newly purchased items with the children. There were four suitcases, already full, sitting in the spare bedroom. By the time she emptied the final two shopping bags, there would be a fifth.

As she folded the new sheer curtains, pulling off the labels, she chuckled, remembering the excitement of her youth decades ago. Brown barrels filled with clothing and food were shipped by relatives to the island aboard ships. In those days, the barrels took a month to reach their destination. Melva was once a child, delighted and on the receiving end of the non-perishable items, clothing, candies, and even an occasional doll. Now, instead of brown barrels, she took a flight in with extra suitcases filled with goodies herself. The children headed to the basement after questioning the purpose of a weird donut cushion and quarreled about whose suitcase it would fit into. Too tired to pack the final items, Melva headed for a hot bath before bed.

"Anything new?" she asked her husband, plopping onto the couch, not wanting to hear somber news tonight but knowing he would repeat it all to her anyway. Her eyes followed the bold letters scrolling across the bottom of the screen and the anchor man's constant droning of breaking announcements. Then, to add to that, there was her phone that was charging for a while. How she hated the constant pinging it emitted when it wasn't tended to.

"Just shut the thing off. Turn it off," would be his response whenever she complained.

The medical correspondent being interviewed stressed the importance of social distancing guidelines as more states saw an uptick in the number of deaths.

"Unfortunately, testing is still very limited and not yet available in many parts of the country." She replied.

"What is the primary reason for the lack of testing kits?"

"Unfortunately, there is a problem with missing parts for the first batch of kits. There were insufficient swabs and the return time on testing was too long," the correspondent stressed.

"How long?"

"Almost ten days. With such delays, many could already be infected and spread the disease to others while waiting for results," the doctor explained.

"This poor woman looks tired," B interjected, "and she could use a brush on that hair."

"This is about the virus, not looks," Melva admonished. "Why can't they just quarantine everyone with suspected symptoms?"

"This is America. You think *you can force dem people in dis country to do dat? Lock up inside?"* He let out a deep belly laugh.

"Well, it's life and death, hon."

"Not for these selfish hooligans. It's all about 'rights and freedoms.' The only virus that can change all the fussin' and protesting is a flesh-eating virus. One that's fast-moving, devouring their flesh and, then you'll see these very same pompous fools voluntarily wrapped up and hiding under their beds, begging for any vaccine to save their hides.

"B, this is not funny. People are dying."

"It's true. I'm serious," he responded, stifling another laugh. "I'm serious. Watch and see. People will not follow rules even if you beg dem. A self-centered bunch you have here."

"Oh, lemme hear what Williamson has to say tonight."

He pressed the remote, poking the buttons as if his life depended on it. Melva was just about deafened by the volume, but at least now she was comfy, ready for bed and, for the first time today, off her feet. She eased into the couch, closing her eyes, knowing that if she started snoring, it would be World War III. He hated noise when his favorite show came on.

"The virus continues to spread unabated, not only in major cities but now more rapidly than before in the midwest and southern states."

On the screen was a map highlighted in shades of red, orange, and yellow zones showing the severity of the spread. Many orange zones were on the rise, dotted throughout the country. The news reporter continued.

"As we speak, there are centers being built adjacent to hospitals to accommodate the influx of patients and those who are homeless. Many hospitals nationwide are making room to accommodate an unprecedented number of infected patients. There were outbreaks in several prisons and nursing homes, spreading weeks before these pockets were identified. This is due to a lack of information, testing, and adherence to the current medical precautionary guidelines."

"And stubborn ignoramuses," B shouted. Melva groaned, turning to her side, eyes closed. "Look who's talking about stubborn. You don't like the mask," she mumbled under her breath.

"It's all overwhelming. We'll be right back with the latest on school protocols, work-from-home trends, and the latest airline updates. Stay tuned."

"Did you stock up on these masks?" He turned to look at her. "I know you're going to kill me if I don't leave the house without three across my face!"

Melva was silent. He glanced over his left shoulder again. She was asleep. He pulled the throw from the end of the couch and covered her shoulders, easing the pillow gently under her head in a futile attempt to stop the impending snoring.

"Sleepyhead, no snoring dearie," he said lovingly. "Looks like we won't be travelin' anytime soon. No getting out, no flyin', no eating out, and no carnival this year. It's way beyond our control," he whispered, humming impromptu to his sleeping wife. He turned the TV off. All was still, including the youngsters upstairs.

CHAPTER 4

Moving the kiddie basketball set and trampoline to the other side of the basement was easy enough, however, there were still a few more bouncy toys to move. This was his quiet man cave for years, but it was totally renovated and carpeted for the children two years ago. The grandchildren kept them busy, and since their parents were stationed overseas, they spent the majority of their time here.

"Too many of these damn toys," B muttered out loud.

I would have been lucky just to have one of those balls. He reminisced about how as a boy, he made toys with friends.

If you wanted a toy, you had to make one like the spinning tops cut out of wood, shaped and fitted with a nail at the bottom and some twine to make them go. The paper kites he remembered fondly, spines fashioned from twigs, sometimes bamboo. The younger boys used cocoa leaves bent at the top, with thread through them. Wax paper was hard to find, so dried leaves worked when necessary. And he wouldn't have had it any other way. Those were happy times spent together, making the most of life with what they had.

Those were the days of fishing in the river, walking miles up in the mountains to collect nutmeg, banana, and cocoa to help feed a family of eight. As the fifth child, he sighed as he remembered the weekly trips carrying bags of produce on his head. In those days, when cars were very few, the nights were pitch black, and electricity was a rarity.

On one of those trips back from the mountains, down the main road, his younger brother, Clifton, was killed coming around the bend close to his home. An oncoming vehicle, one of the few in the village, struck him at dusk as he was running up the hill towards home in the middle of the narrow road. The thought made him tear up. All these years later, he still missed his brother. For years he continued to blame himself for not being there to save him and for wondering why his brother did not hear the engine before the car came around the bend.

They would meet with some of the neighborhood boys on hot days for an outdoor cookout with fresh crawfish, just pulled out from under the river stones nearby. This paired well with dumplings and green bananas. The dumplings were made from flour and a little salt, craftily stolen from an unsuspecting mother. The green lacatan[1] and young bluggoe[2] they picked from the lands of unsuspecting farmers in the vicinity. Whatever ingredients they could find suitable for the soup were handed over by a member of the group. On other days, a loaded fruit tree, whichever was in season, would provide more than enough. There were tough times, and there were times when they teased and filled their bellies with mangoes or other seasonal fruit, easing the burden of their parents. There were many days when mothers could only afford a light dinner of bush tea from local herbs with cheese and crackers. Mealtime was never the same after Clifton died. B would sometimes take crackers from his brother's plate when he wasn't looking and rearranged them to hide his doing. *These grandchildren will probably never know hunger.*

---

1   Type of banana
2   Type of banana

It was a strange year in the quiet village north of the island. A few months later, torrential rains poured down for almost two days. Schools closed, and children stayed indoors. A few men in the village came home that evening to blood running down the side gutters of a steep hill on a street called Alpo. Few neighbors lived there, families that were mostly related. B remembered his father and a few men followed the trail up beneath the nutmeg groves. He remembered the blood, his chest pounding, as he trailed them up the muddy path, hoping he would be allowed to go all the way up the road.

Mr. Nelson turned, looked at the others, and shouted, *"All you know that madman already. I hope he din' do it. That man, I tell you! Gospo got so vexed wid me last month because he catch one of the boys picking up two mangoes over the boundary."*

"Well, Nelson, you know how he greedy, even the goats and his poor donkey, everybody go get a planasse[3] when he get mad. Hope he din' chop up one of them," B's dad shouted over the heavy rainfall.

"Brian, go home, I don't want you to see this. Not sure what we gon see up there," his dad turned, looking sternly in his direction.

"Could be serious. We comin' back soon. Tell your mother, just checking on Gospo."

With that, B turned around towards home. No use arguing with his father, he knew that look: it meant, stay out of grownup's business. He turned around, heading back down towards the main road.

---

3   To hit someone continuously with the broad side of a cutlass which is also known as a machete

They were all drenched. The two men headed up the hill turning into a narrow track leading to Gospo's house. Claps of thunder rumbled in the distance, while the path beneath their feet was brown and muddy. Maybe it was the blood of an animal carcass, a cow perhaps. The water running down the drain was pink now as he ran back toward home.

As he turned the corner, it was already dark. He passed the cocoa trees at the end of the trail. His chest hurting, his tears mingling with the rain, as he remembered his brother's death, hoping his father would be safe, and that everything would be well tonight.

He walked into the little kitchen through the back door. The kerosene lamp offered some welcoming light. His mother did not quarrel. Instead, she listened silently, as he blurted out the day's events. She asked no questions, just groaned, shaking her head when he mentioned Mr. Gospo. As he devoured a leftover bake from breakfast, crackers and saltfish with his younger siblings for supper, he finally heard some commotion outdoors. He could hear his father's booming voice, conversing, up the steps to the kitchen door. His mom quickly opened it, looking worried, with a towel in hand. His father stood at the door.

"Clara, he killed his wife."

What?" His mother leaned sideways as his father steadied her.

"Look like he chop her up and throw her in dat dam. We called for him, knocked, no answer. That was where most of the blood was comin' from. Noel's Dam. We went to look. The neighbor went down to try to get the police. Don't know how long."

"Why would he do dat? Why?" His mom could not hold back the tears. B still remembered these incidents as if they had happened yesterday. A certain air of tragedy fell upon them all when he first heard the news. Life is something! His mind raced through his migration, the slights at the plant, the slow climb. Thank God he was able to retire before all this.

"Papa, I'm home!" The enthusiastic greeting interrupted his thoughts. He turned to see his granddaughter at their basement door, excited to get to her indoor playground. He swallowed hard, hugging her as she ran in.

"There's my girl! Where are the others?"

"No school tomorrow," Mya shouted twirling across the playroom.

"What?" He feigned disbelief.

"And no school next week either."

"Don't believe you."

"OK, ask Troy when he comes down."

This pandemic was causing more disruption than they had ever imagined. Now the children would be home indefinitely. He made his way upstairs and greeted his grandson.

"Let me guess, no school tomorrow?" He cocked his head with a straight face.

"Ha, ha, and we had to use hand sanitizer and masks. The bus monitor says we should use it all the time."

"OK, son, I hear you," B chuckled. Now his wife, as well as his grandchildren, were disease control experts, and he was in the direct line of fire. He followed the rules, but now it would be *extra* as the kids would say. Things were about to get rough around here. He chuckled as Troy squeezed passed him with a wide grin on his face.

CHAPTER 5

"Welcome back to our daily briefing. We have Dr. Paige, an infectious disease expert on our panel this evening. We also have our CDC correspondent Dr. Johnson to bring us the latest update on the number of cases and the rapid expansion of testing. We welcome you both to the show."

Clyde and Sherie, the next-door neighbors, stopped in for a quick visit and both families were glued to the daily briefing already in progress.

"Pandemic. In my lifetime, never heard of such a thing. It's just a big hullabaloo to make these pharmaceutical companies more bucks if you ask me," Clyde shouted. "It can't be that serious."

"Hush, let me hear what these turkeys have to say," Sherie looked over, annoyed at her hubby, suddenly wishing he would zip it. B looked at the two of them, turning up the volume.

"Dr. Paige, what should the public be aware of at this time? Give us the latest updates."

"Thank you for having me. Use the standard precautions. Avoid large crowds, if you are compromised or have any co-morbidities. If you are elderly, use extra precautions. Keep social distancing guidelines, six feet if possible, and wear a mask. If you can, in the areas where testing is readily available, please get tested if you have any of the known symptoms or if you have been in contact with anyone who is positive."

"Doctor, what are the symptoms for those who are not aware?"

"This virus in humans presents as body aches, pain in the lower extremities and joints, diarrhea in some, loss of taste, chills, fever, and headaches. Some may have, in rare cases, experienced brain fog and hallucinations. Please contact your primary care physician if you have any of these symptoms. If you do not have a physician and are experiencing severe symptoms and problems with breathing, please go to the nearest emergency room in your area."

"Is it safe for people to go into the clinics?"

"Please call first to schedule an appointment. Do not present to your clinic without an appointment."

"Sherie, you said last night that you had pain in your knees and ankles. Present yourself?" Clyde chuckled, looking over at his wife.

"You know it's arthritis. This is no joke. People are dying, and the numbers keep going up."

"It's revenge of the 'Rona that's killing people," he replied.

Dr. Johnson continued, "As of this hour, stats reporting today are one hundred forty-three deaths and over six thousand more positive cases in this city alone."

"Why the sudden climb in numbers?" The news anchor questioned, staring intently at the expert directly across the desk, referencing the graph on the screen behind.

"Well, it was the height of this past holiday weekend, the crowds, and travel. Also, the guidelines were initially ignored for the most part during the beginning stages. Keep in mind that our testing was also delayed due to lack of supplies."

"I bet you those rich folks in the hills had extra kits and supplies," B muttered. "No missing swabs up in the suburbs."

The anchor shook his head in disbelief. "Dr. Paige, what about the labs? And the delays with results, sometimes up to two entire weeks?" His eyes were large and red from hours of continuous pandemic coverage.

"Most labs were not equipped to deal with the onslaught of testing on such a large scale, and there were initial logistical issues with coordination on the national levels. This is an event we could not have anticipated, and we are doing the best we can to overcome these temporary hiccups. Due to more robust coordination efforts in the past week, I am glad to share that we are now moving forward more cohesively and robustly."

"What about the latest advisories for this quarantine?"

"Melva, you and these people want to lock me up?" B groaned, knowing that more rules were in order.

"Keep joking. We'll see," she replied.

"I bet she must have stocked up the closets already with the pandemic wipes…umm, bleach, vitamin tonics, antiviral toilet tissue, pandemic oils, eh!" Clyde joked.

"Man, hush, I want to hear," Sherie shot him yet another side-eye.

B and Mel lost their right to silence whenever they came over.

"Global pandemic my foot. This thing is just to get poor people out of their homes. It's all about real estate in these cities. Bet real estate sales are booming in some places while evictions are looming for us." Clyde continued.

The show was about to wrap. The safety guidelines were scrolling up in bold with a reminder to check the site for any additional information.

Those using mass transit should be cautious and wear their masks at all times.

Schools will remain closed indefinitely.

Gyms, bars, theaters, and churches will remain closed until further notice.

Six feet is the recommended distancing guideline.

Self-quarantine from family members if infected.

CHAPTER 6

"Not one damn egg in the grocery store, not even at that big overpriced market," said the angry senior leaving the counter, pointing his cane towards the refrigerators against the far wall as he exited the bodega.

"Lady, would you tell me when the next truck comes in? I need some toilet paper. Do you have any?" He turned slowly sideways, glaring at the cashier.

"Truck comes first thing in the morning. If you come about 10:30, Mr. Ralph, we should have eggs and toilet paper when it comes. I'll save some for you, promise."

"Lady, what time did you say? 10:30?"

"Yes, the truck comes around that time. It only comes once a week now because there are not enough drivers."

"Need those damn eggs. I'll be here. Yeah, and I'm gonna need to wipe my butt too," he grumbled, carrying two grocery bags in one free hand and his cane in the other as he limped onto the busy sidewalk. He was a widower. A fixture in the neighborhood who walked the same three blocks every few days to replenish what little he could carry and afford on his limited income.

Marissa looked at him as he exited and felt sorry for him, less for herself. In no time, it was a challenge to do anything. Getting a car battery was an act of congress, so was scheduling a doctor's appointment, finishing a class, getting wipes or taking an exam. These basic choices all seemed to evaporate within the last month. Marisa needed the job, and her two children were ordered to stay out of school indefinitely due to this virus. This caused a last-minute scramble to find care for the rambunctious pair for the unforeseen future.

"I'll do it," Ms. V offered, "I'm not worried one bit." Marissa knew this was against the COVID-19 guidelines for a 70-something to mingle with her kids, or any other kids for that matter. But she needed the help, and Mrs. V needed the money, so they brokered a symbiotic deal.

"I'm not worried about this here foolishness. These fools don't know their ass from their elbow, or they would have this virus under control. It's controlling them. Bring the boys in the morning, I'll be up early."

"Thank you so much. You don't know how much it means," Marissa gave a sigh of relief.

"And don't bother to feed them. I have enough," Mrs. V punctuated.

Marissa stifled a laugh, a reminder that she had to pack breakfast foods and snacks with the boys in the morning as their bottomless stomachs would empty Mrs. V's pantry by midday that very first day. For years, Mrs. V kept children on and off. She needed to for home expenses. Her modest retirement check, a modest pension from her husband and her social security could not sometimes handle all the monthly expenses.

The fact that the four-bedroom, two-story house was in decent condition and able to pass the mandatory state inspection was a blessing. With a finished basement, there was ample room for her to keep a few kids at a time. Her husband left her a newly renovated lovely home after he died. It was the best one on the block at the time. In the couple's heyday, when she wore furs, they had matching outfits and drove a fine car. They were a part of the Black northern migration, and they fared better up here and were proud of what they had accomplished. Now, with gentrification, many of her neighbors sold their homes and moved away; she was determined to stay.

The three-storied brownstone still looked grand on the outside. They had no children of their own, but she was grateful that they were together until the day he died. Their relationship survived the wagging tongues of a childless marriage and a few affairs on both sides. She was not afraid to entertain Marissa and anyone who would listen. Marissa loved the story about the time she threw a "bold, narrow hussy with a dried-up wig" out of their attic bedroom window. She returned home unexpectedly one night from a family visit to Georgia and was livid. She seemed to exhibit amnesia somehow and always omitted her husband's role and fate in these colorful tales.

"Yes, the older one has a deep pit of a stomach with a milk addiction. I will bring cereal with them in the morning," Marissa reiterated. With that, the deal was sealed before anyone else could take those precious two slots.

The subway was sparse these days, and it felt more like a Sunday morning when she picked the boys up in the evening after work.

It seemed like it would be their last day at the afterschool program for the unforeseen future. She had to fight to get them to keep those stifling masks on. It would have to be a food bribe for the moment. These were the times when she remembered her mother's words, a thin no-nonsense woman with little patience for rambunctious children.

"Always keep beans in your pantry and a bone. Soup will feed your family for days," she would always say. These words rang so true now because some foods were just plain hard to find these days, and prices were steadily rising, keeping up with inflation. She thanked her lucky stars; the boys ate anything in sight.

The ride home was still. The train cars were sparse, but the boys were engrossed in their screens with no worries of adulthood on their minds. Twice during the ride home, she made them rub their palms with sanitizer. In return, they gave her a crazy look and turned around to see if anyone was watching. The cool air greeted them as they climbed up the stairs from Avenue station. It was already dark as they braced for a brisk, two-block walk to their home.

CHAPTER 7

"You can't come down to see us for just a few days? What if you book the flight today? There is one every day, right? You mean they really closed the airports up there?" Aunty Lou shouted into the phone.

"Tanty,[4] listen, there are no flights from here and none from most countries until further notice. We have to wait until there is some control of this virus," I replied for the second time in less than five minutes.

"But girl, a flight just came in today."

"Not from up here. We're not accepted. Guess we're contaminated. It's the rules, Tanty." I knew the island would not accept flights from here, but I did not want to alarm her.

"Baby, it would be safer here in these parts, you know that. Wish you were here. We only have a few cases of the virus compared to up there." Few cases," she chuckled.

"I'll be OK. Classes will continue online, but the entire family is moving upstate, so I have to move with them."

"Where are they moving?"

"Marsdale area, about an hour from the city."

"Oh?" I sensed her worry.

"Yes," I shouted, "The Mrs. thinks it would be safer up there for the boys, so I am helping pack up stuff for the kids to take. You know she makes all the decisions."

---

4   Term for Aunt

"OK, well, that sounds like a lot on top of your studies, dear."

"It is, but it's flexible, and it pays, you know. Plus, it's temporary. Just filling in for my friend."

"I do, dear. Well, call me and let me know when you get up there." I could detect some stress in her lilting accent despite the casual conversation. She was happily retired, and there was no way to get her back here, not even for a visit.

"I will, and the mail is so slow now. Let me know if you all need anything; it will probably be a month longer."

"Girl, I hear they stopped the mail, local and foreign. Mailman did not come this week."

"OK, don't worry about it. I have to go, will call you on the weekend. Love you."

I quickly said my goodbyes and switched gears to the tasks that lay ahead.

As I packed the twin blue hard suitcases with clothing and the crates with toys, I looked at the lengthy list Luanne requested to be loaded into their SUV, wondering how it could all be possible. I was awakened last night just after submitting an overdue assignment on global tourism and its effects on island nations. The phone pinged in rapid succession, and I knew that it would be an early rising. There were several segments, somehow out of order, with lists of how and what to pack for the boys - enough to last at least two weeks. There was no thank you, no please, and void of the usual smiley emojis. I only took the job to help a friend who felt bad about leaving the country for the semester and did not want to leave them stranded. It helped that the pay was really good, though. *It would only be for a while*, I comforted myself.

Ping

"For the safety of the family, we all need to get out of the city."

Ping

"Sorry for the short notice hope you won't mind."

Ping

"Your classes are all online now?"

Ping

"When you get in, just finish packing the orange crate."

Ping

"A head start, yay. I've already packed the drones and large toys for both."

Even in my tired stupor, I understood that "we" did not include any input from her husband, Bill, by any stretch of the imagination. It was as if Bill and the boys were a mere afterthought in most of her plans, crammed into a cluttered corner of Luanne's mind. The media coverage was fueling her already spastic tendencies. I dove further under the warm quilt, pulling it over my head and sinking into my small pillow, the ultra-soft one. *I must bring it with me tomorrow.* I reminded myself before sleep swirled me back in with the hum of the heater in the background. I had a few precious hours. *A lot was uncomfortable up there. Maybe I could just find a way to get out of this tomorrow?* Maybe.

CHAPTER 8

"Morning! I've already had the exterior disinfected, got the door handles, the cabinets and the screens," Luanne barged into the boys' closet, waving the spray can as I started on the large yellow crate, trying my best to focus on the tasks at hand, but it was impossible for anyone to tune her out. I thought of my mother and what she must have endured on her job in trying times like these.

"Well, what if a real flesh-eating plague came on the heels of this one? What would these stupid people do?" would have been her blunt reply to this fiasco. I remained silent, remembering our last conversation before she died. She thought the world was changing way too fast and not for the better. There would be other contagions in these times, pestilence, and plague would unleash, according to the scriptures.

"The knee pads, where are they?" I rummaged through a bin in the corner, talking to myself. That would be the hardest thing to find in their rooms now. Poor Bill and those boys, they probably got no sleep last night. At least there was a few hours left before we all would head out of the city today after completing all those tasks.

Bill greeted me with a sheepish grin. His bald spot was covered with a perfunctory comb-over of thin blond hair and bags under his eyes. He left the sanctuary of his study for a break from the constant cloud of disinfectant spray aimed in his direction.

"Good, you're here," he dodged, covering his nose as the Mrs. was walking the hall again, spray can in hand.

"Yes." I chuckled. We could hear the closet door at the end of the hall open. My jacket was being disinfected. The heavy linen scent made my empty stomach churn. He lifted both his arms apologetically, silent, his eyes big. I stifled a moan.

"Coffee?" he asked.

"Yes, thanks."

The bed was covered with items that could not possibly fit in the two suitcases. Both boys lay on their twin beds, oblivious to the commotion. Josh's blond spiked hair was visible, and his face was buried in his pillow. Alex was silent, zoned into his blue tablet.

There were two jars of disinfecting wipes next to a backpack on the bed. I grabbed them and tossed both into the duffle bag on the floor. The Mrs. would probably use them all up before the end of the drive out of the city today.

I paused, staring out at the floor-to-ceiling windows ahead, taking a sip from the cup Bill handed to me. I walked towards them, looking down below at the eerily quiet avenues no longer bustling with traffic and milling crowds. We were all exhausted and confused.

Breaking news spouted from the screen into the den that overlooked the park below. It seemed this was the only respite, looking out at the skyscrapers or way down to the green expanse, the only nature reserve in this area of the city. I felt foggy and anxious about the weeks ahead, my schedule, and the family in the room around me.

It's not like there was nothing at the other house. It made me mad to know so many children were doing without. Evictions were pending at an all-time high. The basement upstate held gaming and outdoor equipment, lots of it. I already heard that from the boys and Bill. Luanne demanded too much of these items. Now, I had to find the flavored toothpaste.

The smell of bleach was thick. I bolted back out; this meant that the cleaning lady came already today, at the crack of dawn. Everything was spotless. I bet she doubled up on Rosa's pay this month in exchange for days of deep cleaning. Good. She needed the money.

"This lady is way, way too picky!" Rosa complained to me a few weeks ago as I walked in for my shift. She was leaving the high-rise luxury apartment building on her way to another job two blocks away on the avenue.

"I understand," I mumbled, hoping to stay out of it.

"You know, she has these lists and keeps adding. I have other places to clean." I nodded again.

"I don't have that problem anywhere else. Been doing this for over five years. How do you work with her being new and everything?" she asked. I shrugged silently. For me, it was temporary, as with everything else these days.

I left the suitcases and a large duffle in the hall for Bill to take down to the elevators and turned slowly, scanning the area for any favorite particulars of the children. I headed to the bathroom with my phone to have a break. *Finally*. I closed the door with a sigh of relief. As I sat on the edge of the tub, the fan on blast, I bent over, staring at the screen, and I felt my spine relax for the first time that day. I scrolled up. The feeds of the death toll had doubled from the week before.

Now, the governor would be rolling out new rules of enforcement intended to keep the population safe. The nursing homes were a direct hit. There was no respite in sight.

"Wonder if that would work?" I muttered out loud as I flushed again, closed my eyes for another few minutes, and flushed again—*no time to send messages now*. I thought of the thinning subway traffic and the sparse city street void of bustling pedestrians. Now, there were actual seats on the train during rush hour, yes, lots of them. More people were wearing masks. I sometimes wore mine, but now it was going to be necessary according to the guidelines. Last week, I lied when my bossy friend Diedra asked me if I had my mask on the way home.

I checked the new state-by-state tracker, showing how fast the spread was in some parts of the country. Hopefully, the Mrs. did not get her eyes on this tracker yet. I couldn't handle her seismic spasms, not today. I got up after five minutes, washed my hands, and thanked the creator that there were three bathrooms in this apartment for days like these.

"Here, guys, come eat your sandwiches." I bribed the boys with anything containing cheese. It worked and kept them full and quiet while I checked my inbox for the latest assignment from my instructor. They ate the entire thing and went back to their entertainment while I speedily read a chapter on the prevalence of online sex trafficking.

CHAPTER 9

Josh giggled in the back seat, leaning over to show his younger brother another funny video.

"Look at this."

I heard a familiar jingle of the quarantine kind, ad nauseam.

"She can't dance!" Alex shouted, looking up.

"Yeah, but the talking dog can. Look at his ears. He wants to be let out," Josh roared.

"What's that?" Alex asked.

"A matching eye patch, silly." The music changed as Josh swiped again.

"Oh, that lady got so mad. The bear suit scared her shitless," Josh whispered.

"No way. I don't ever wanna see this again," Alex replied. They both giggled again.

Alex was comfortable with his older brother but was usually silent and buried in his tablet. He had an advantage being the younger of the two. He mastered a way of zoning both parents out ninety percent of the time, leaving most of the burden of parental anxiety to his older brother. I, too, fell into the role of buffering the elder from the endless griping of one parent and the emotional exhaustion of the other.

With several suitcases and crates, all five of us managed to cram into the shiny black SUV and were well on our way upstate. The tree-lined roads were almost empty, as we left the lights, noise and skyscrapers behind for at least a week.

There was one assignment looming despite the national disaster, and this would be my only time to skim over the materials before doing the assigned report. My earbuds were jammed in my ear, the only effective do-not-disturb weapon against the whole clan. I glanced sideways to the passenger front seat, noticing Luanne was slumped to one side, asleep for the moment. Bill was focused on getting us to point B in record time, silently praying, we were sure to get there before she awoke.

I scrolled through the pages of chapter twelve of the text and turned up the volume to drown out the boys' laughter. I wondered *how in the world do these kids get millions of followers with these silly memes, dragging their dances, dogs, grandmas, and anything goofy into these videos?* I was only halfway through the dense chapter, and I knew I couldn't complete it in time. *I will have to recall the earlier chapters I'd already browsed.* Distracted, I swiped through the latest feeds. Masks were now mandated nationwide for outdoor activities beginning tomorrow, with very few exceptions. Every week, there would be a new buzz phrase to go along with whatever new recommendations were given.

I swiped again. There were several protests in major cities earlier in the day. There was a large group of protestors somewhere in the heartland dead set against this new mandate. Two men held up a large red sign leading their cause, "Hungry. Open restaurants now." followed by another, "We are all essential."

More feeds meant more complaints, one of which featured a few parents gathered to discuss the stay-at-home policy and its effects on working parents. An irate mother explained on video that the week before, she had to quit work to take care of the full-time needs of her children. Another gave warnings of spreading wildfires on the west coast, with no end in sight. Responders from other parts of the country were being sent in to squelch the blazes, which were spreading by leaps and bounds. "Masks: A Double Necessity" was the title of a young, overworked healthcare provider's article recommending dual masking. Then there were the loud complaints about governmental restrictions and the right to be mask free. *What would be next?* The feeds were unrelenting, but I could not look away. I needed to, soon, or it would be a surefire path to depression.

"Update: Pastor Arrested for Molestation and Embezzlement," I couldn't swipe anymore. My eyes burned as I stopped to scan the piece. There were several cash exchanges between a wife, a lover, and an underaged male, who came forward with his parents to tell his story. I closed my eyes, my fingers pressing the buttons on the side of the phone, rendering the screen black. *Damn! Really?* I raised my head to peek across at both boys, who had also fallen asleep peacefully. So far, looks like they were going through this time unbothered.

The streets were dark during the latter part of the journey that featured tall pines, winding roads, and no houses. It would be about half an hour left to our destination. I pulled my sweater up and around my shoulders and sunk into the seat with an uneasy coziness. The hum of the vehicle was a sedative, momentarily drowning out the impending chaos of our arrival.

BLOG II - MY COUNTRY

This sense of entitlement will come crashing down soon enough. A country filled to the brim with lofty, self-centered ideas of what is best for the individual. It's all about the superior, ME and MINE and a very selective WE.

No one can make me wear a damn mask! Why can't I go wherever the hell I want to go? Why can't the restaurants open up, and why can't they deliver when I want them to? Why can't I travel abroad in this crisis and treat people where I go with disrespect and still expect great hospitality?

Why do we need law and order when we have law and order, our appointed court justices, and the laws that we approve. We'll have order after all, we stormed the capital, ransacked the desks, assaulted police, citizens, hurled racial slurs and re-branded the entire fiasco as a peaceful protest. It's our country, after all, OURS.

And if you don't teach the version of history we created and that we've always taught, we're coming for you. We'll decide on the right curriculum. Yes, we know what is best for the country and the entire world. The truth. As for truth, we define truth as we've seen it. We've always defined truth. Why do you people want to start division? There was no division before. There was no division before in this country, because I said so.

WE will make policy for you in your city without even consulting your so called officials. We don't care about lack of resources and broken infrastructure, that's not OUR responsibility. WE don't have to sit down with you, even though we are in the same state in OUR country. And WE will expel you from office if you don't think exactly like US, revel in our ideas even to the detriment of your community and constituents. And while you're at it, we expect you to dress like US, get approval from US and change your hair and features to look like us, because WE are the only ones, perfect, created in God's image. WE can be polite to you, smile and be accomodating, but internally when you walk in a room, we know we are superior, we were programmed that way for centuries. WE are sure of it and continue to perpetuate it, in OUR schools and curriculum, and your schools too. WE will block any attempts, with fervor to change that programming.

WE are omnipotent and omniscient and make no mistakes. See our great history? Even though we run the state, and this city is a part of OUR state and is failing miserably, it's not our fault, never, that there are not enough resources in those parts. The colossal health crisis? There is no real crisis in our area of the state. WE are concerned about that Fentanyl though, it has been a crisis for US for some time now.

Let me watch the game in peace. Don't bother me with your problem and injustice protests and taking a knee in the middle of MY pastime. Even the players are mine when I want them to be.

And why is this other political party still in existence? Only one party should exist, and my people live near me in my neighborhood. I should be able to shoot anyone—kill them for that matter, if they come walking through in MY neighborhood, My trees, my dirt, grass, my air, the sun is mine, my clouds, stars and stripes. I will change borders at any time in history to fit my needs. That's what MY America is supposed to be! Why are you arresting these men for killing that Black man? They were protecting their neighborhood.

I did not reread it, but this would be a great piece for discussion at the next meetup. I saved it and put it on the calendar as a reminder. *The answers to these questions posed never come easy for any society. It takes a national or global whiplash, painful and traumatic, as history has shown, to be stripped of privilege and pride. The ones who are lucky enough to survive will have the collective injuries as a lesson in humility. And that resulting limp will be a constant reminder of how to live in this world.*

CHAPTER 10

"Well, no one can come in or fly out anywhere!" Tanty moaned into the phone. Travel plans were postponed indefinitely since most islands restricted any flights from leaving or coming into their single airports. The precautions were necessary due to limited medical resources and small hospitals.

"What about Jerard, out there on that cruise ship?" I asked. He was a cousin who worked for over four years with one of the major cruise lines and was due to be home after a six-month contract. With a wife and young child and aunty next door to take care of, his absence was sorely missed. I knew because I heard about it every time my aunt got a chance to talk about it.

"Girl, he's stuck in quarantine too. The ship did not come in last weekend. He said they would all have to stay for at least another week dealing with all those stranded 'cruisers.' It's for everyone's safety, I hope they will get home somehow."

"Well, it's not good for anyone to be stranded out there this long. People have families and responsibilities. Send them home." I gritted my teeth at this unending global drama. Everyone was feeling it.

"Tanty, nobody knows how long and even if he is allowed to disembark, he can't even come in. What I understood is that they must remain in quarantine another seven days after arriving in a local hotel before being sent home."

"Girl, the whole world shut down for one little plague. Everybody's up in arms now. What if there was another one?"

Her accent deepened as she delved into the current neighborhood gossip, the latest titillating story that she was so passionate about. I could picture her next to the window, looking out at the hedges with the bright birds of paradise nearby. In the distance, the tall dark green peaks ahead, her voice within earshot of her neighbor. Next to the hibiscus hedges on the left were a few sugarcane plants in the corner, her "crayfish cane," referring to a type of plant with a green and white exterior. I kept a picture of her, smiling, in a bright yellow dress, right hand on her hip, the perfect complement to her dark skin. Her salt and pepper 'fro was short, natural and on point, as she liked it.

This sugarcane was a sober reminder of why we were citizens on this side of the world. Our ancestors were robbed of their rightful heritage, genealogical family line, and place, all for sugar—an unnecessary commodity, reaping havoc on the health of our people to this day. She smiled, standing slender and tall against the lush backdrop where our enslaved fore-parents toiled to produce for that terrible triangle, providing limitless profits for the British. These plantation owners profited then and were later compensated again by their rulers at the end of slavery for their losses, after emancipation, imagine that. Yet whatever shore we landed on, our lives would be present and future witnesses for all the families who did not survive the middle passage. They were the ones who were murdered, treated like animals, stacked like sardines, suffered through terror, sickness, starvation, and thrown overboard in the ocean route. This, was the reality of the Triangle of the trans-Atlantic slave trade, a reign of terror many hope to move on and forget. But how can we, as one people, created in the image and likeness of the Creator, just forget?

We are the descendants, proud survivors, and thrivers who are descendants of tortured African hostages. We are pawns in a greedy, limitless loot for nature's bounty, world domination, and endless monetary profits; greed. Profits in the tropical paradise and others nearby, where my aunt took this photo, were of sugar and salt. The volcanic peaks that Tanty could see from her window were so far silent but could erupt when they were ready. Like the one on the neighboring island recently did, sending ash hundreds of miles away, blanketing all in its path. That one gave little warning before it belched and vomited over the island, causing financial ruin for many local farmers. The neighboring islands offered respite by opening their doors to help while the volcano was active. Most, however, chose not to evacuate.

"I have to tell you this!" she chuckled. My neighbor down the road offered to take up to six women into his home, but despite his generous offer, nobody showed up in his yard yet," she cackled with delight. Her curtains would be drawn back if it was a breezy day, her chickens scratching in the dirt under the nutmeg trees in the backyard.

She hated traveling by herself, embarking just once to see Uncle B and Mel, and a second time to a sister island to see her brother whom she missed.

"You pay all this money for high walls, concrete, and bad air," she would say when she missed family and wanted to put us on a guilt trip.

"I'm not coming back up there! No view, no breeze, and it's freezin'," she continued. The worst was the food as she was unimpressed with all four restaurants she visited.

"These people dunno[5] about cooking. Best food is right from this kitchen." She was right about that.

---

5 Don't know

Jerard lived around the bend from Tanty with his girlfriend, Val, and young son when he was not on the ship. I asked about Val, unable to avoid the impending drama.

"The poor girl worry, worry every day. I wonder what else to do for her. Poor ting[6]." Then she told me of the two deaths, not of COVID-19, but of an elderly lady with dementia and another young girl with a heart problem, before returning to the topic.

"She's holding up for the time being since he's stranded and can't come home. I gave her something last week to help out. She came here crying about missing him and said she wasn't sleeping. She says she sees things in the backyard at night. When six o'clock comes, she shuts all her blinds tight. I dunno about that girl sometimes."

"She's just stressed, Tanty, you all just worry warts. She's worse than you."

"Tania, gurl, I tell you I seen' spirits in me yard? Did I tell you I see tings at night?"

"No, but you believe in La Diablesse, Mama Malady, and Ligaroo and who knows what else." I chuckled, remembering the childhood stories of the Ligaroo. He was a scraggly, blood-sucking man that turned into a spirit, flew into your bedroom and sucked your blood, leaving a spot on your arm or torso so you could see the evidence the next morning. The La Diablesse was supposedly a spirit woman with one hoof and one good foot. She lured men in with her good looks. As a child, I was not afraid of her because as a girl, I knew she would leave me alone. There were many colorful tales of these figures, but we would have to discuss them another day. She loved to tell them, and they were delightful when she explained the details. Mama Malady was the sick lady who traveled at night, on the

---

6   Thing

lookout for anyone she could find. I did not understand why a sick lady would be up at night looking for anyone. Maybe I had them all mixed up, I heard so many of these stories.

"Girl, hush."

"Did La Diablese get rid of her hoof?" I loved to tease her. "Where is her good foot, Tanty? The Ligaroo sucked off her toes?"

We both laughed. I knew she believed those island stories. The ones I loved to listen to as a little girl just before bed, when it was pitch dark while the insects' sounds pierced through the still night on the island.

Despite her complaining, she was glad to have neighbors, and family close by and was not happy that most of the family left the country years ago. She busied herself with her kitchen garden, planting tomatoes in neat beds, pigeon peas, manioc[7] and dasheen. She was proud of how many pumpkins were on the vine this year.

"Send me a picture?" I chuckled, knowing her frustration.

"Can't understand these damn phones. Will get Val to send dem[8] pictures for you."

"What did you do with your phone?"

"The screen always gets dark all of a sudden. I can't handle pushing this and swiping that."

"I understand. Well, I have to head out now. You know how it is around here." It was my usual cue to end the conversation.

"Just make sure when Paul delivers the groceries from the store to wipe them down first, even the bottles," I reminded her.

"Yes, dear. Will do."

"Love you."

---

7   Cassava. An edible root.
8   The

"Love you too. Call me on the weekend. Bye." She lived in about the best location in the world for this present situation, I thought as I headed out to the store.

CHAPTER 11

The smoke from the tear gas filled the screen, obscuring the protesters in front of the station. The mayor was present earlier that day, at different times, in support of thousands of people tired of the blatant, systemic racism in law enforcement and policing tactics spanning hundreds of years. Just last week there was a news report about a few well-established Black businessmen who could not secure loans at local banks even though the federal government allotted the funds to assist with the current crises. In the meantime, their white counterparts had little or no problems securing loans. The study showed that this happened in several states, and there were no explanations for the results, except for systemic racism firmly rooted in the fabric of this society. Some farmers came out too. Black farmers, some new including a rare few who owned farms for generations, specifically brought into focus details of their accounts of persistent negative outcomes with banks for over a century in this country.

There were housing protestors. There were parents demanding clean water, fresh produce and safe schools. The list kept growing, but officials were not listening. There was an outcry in response to some crafty gerrymandering officials who were hell-bent on slicing and dicing up districts in closed-door meetings in hopes of diluting some votes. These seasoned strategic secretive schemers hoped to avoid future consequences in court.

"Vote them out," they chanted.

This pandemic awakened a sense of responsibility in some citizens to try to understand why these large crowds were gathering in the streets—and why now. The crowds swelled from all creeds, conditions, and walks of life. They came in support, some with far-reaching, alternate agendas, but nonetheless, they showed up in one great swell. Well into the evening the crowds continued marching. Even the curfew or national guards could not stop the growing swell, exposing the underside of a broken democracy for the world to see.

"Why is everyone so sensitive these days? You can't even say anything. This division is not good for our country." That was the perfunctory response on the nightly news from those who felt it an annoyance or a distraction. It was not in their best interest to even take the time out of their privileged zones to understand.

"We're all American," was the standard response of those who refused to see.

"But whose America? There is a divide, a difference in our experiences in this country." The reporter questioned an agitated blond woman who presented the safe all-American response.

"Well, I don't understand this protest. All our lives matter every day."

"Well, some lives are in much greater jeopardy in this country, and what we are witnessing is another movement for change."

"I don't understand it, really," she frantically pulled her hair from her face.

"Understanding and equality are what we must embrace if we want to live peaceably," her daughter responded loudly into the mic. They were a family apparently divided by generation about the realities facing this country.

The protesters started running toward the sidewalk as uniformed guards and police marched in from three sides to dismantle the protests. Unmarked cars also lined the far end of the park in the distance. The crowds continued to face the police, who had created a human shield slowly advancing towards the sidewalk. The camera zoomed into a sea of signs carried by the protestors.

"Get your feet off our backs!"

"I am a man." A young Black man held up his sign, reminiscent of protests and photos from decades past. "Another century, same shit." was another slogan his friend was carrying. The story was playing out like an old classic movie, dusted off and replayed in a country that refused to acknowledge a problem, cancer from within that was showing symptoms, eating away and spreading inwards. Yet, simultaneously, all signs are, for the time being, ignored.

A family carried two signs. One of which was carried by the young children in tow.

"Our house is crumbling!"

"Let's fix it."

Three couples looked on at the unrest from the large screen mounted on the far wall of a large sunroom surrounded by falling leaves and a cool breeze. They were lifelong friends for decades, went to school together and lived in the same town as their parents did before them.

"I don't understand all this—in a pandemic?" Charlie mused, putting up the cards, a weekly ritual at his home.

"Well, dear, people are frustrated. No money and time on their hands, so..." his wife Jane trailed off.

"It's been festering for a long time. Remember the California riots in the nineties? The same incidents keep happening to this day. It's time for a reckoning now. People are just so tired, and rightfully so." Unlike his friends, Jim was the most vocal and in tune with current policies and undercurrents.

"I remember when we were young," Jane interjected, "we lived down the street from a Black family. I didn't see race when I was growing up, still don't, can't understand it for the life of me."

"You won't and can't," Jim responded, "because it is irrelevant to you. You don't experience the level of discrimination they do."

"What do you mean?" She seemed offended, raising her wine glass for another swig.

"Charlie," she looked at her husband to come to her defense. "I see what goes on; I've worked in foster care for years. These poor children, foster care, and broken homes. Do you know the pain these kids go through and the cost to the state?"

"Dear, I know you have experience with children, but we don't feel what they feel, dear. We don't get treated like second-class citizens everywhere and every day. Remember the interview with that Black track star last week?"

"Well am I racist for saying that? I just don't see color, and I help when I can," she responded.

"You have to see color." Jim turned to face the couple. "If you call yourself God-fearing people, you have to see color. The way God created us, he created them. You can't just ignore it. Color matters in this society and in this scheme we created all over the damn world. It's the backbone of so many societies. Call it caste, class, or colorism, it's all a festering pile of prejudice. You think no one is responsible for it?"

"Well, I'll be darned," Tammy responded in alarm. Usually quiet, she stood up. "Now we're bringing religion into this malarkey."

"Yes, we are. If we are all children of God, when some continue to suffer, we can't sit in perpetual comfort and just relax in color-blind oblivion for our convenience!" Jim lifted his hands, stating what he felt should be obvious.

"Well, I see the point," she sighed. Wilbur, and his wife Jane, who was recovering from surgery, remained silent, with strained looks on their faces through the entire discussion.

They were all aggravated now, like they had been before last week when the initial protests made headline news. A sudden silence blanketed the sunroom, where their grandchildren used to play in perpetual safety. Pickles, the fluffy Maine Coon, sunned himself in the corner oblivious to the conundrums of the group. The cleaning lady hated Pickles because his fur blanketed everything in his path. She could not stand him. He made her want to quit and tell them to invest in a damn robot cleaner to trap all that fur.

****

It's so hard for people to understand what someone is going through when things don't personally affect them or their family. Then, whatever happens, is not relevant. Even after a sermon on loving thy neighbor, they still don't get it. It must be a superiority complex when it comes to who God is and who his beloved is too. We say one God, but not really. Looks like the view of us as his children can't register in their unyielding minds. I see it here with Luanne and her husband and kids. Her thoughts take precedence and spill out without regard. She would scheme, whine and complain just to get her way; total manipulation of all members of the family. If this happens in a family, it can occur in a country. We see it all the time.

I'm so damn tired, but most of us are voiceless even when we hold up signs that people can clearly read and understand. Even as we get beaten, stomped on, demoted, passed up, jailed, evicted, and made fun of. But don't worry. It usually takes a dramatic event for permanent change to pan into view. History tells us as much. The problem is that some of us are not built for dramatic events. When one occurs, we can't survive. Pills and refills won't do the trick then. Funny it'll come, it never fails.

The Tired One

CHAPTER 12

Uncle B took pride in trimming his hedges. He loved a square hedge with sharp edges at the sidewalk, with two large, round shrubs in the middle. Finally, there was a rectangle at the foot of the steps that headed up to the front door. His neighbor and retirement buddy, Joe, looked on somewhat amused from his adjoining porch next door.

B paused and turned around with a puzzled look on his face.

"Did you hear about those large wasps?" he asked as the thought crossed his mind.

"Yeah, heard something about those giant hornets. They came out of nowhere. But where you think they came from man?" Joe asked, screwfaced.

"Was about a week ago. I heard it was in another state, forget which one, came in from overseas. They're just spreading man," B took aim at the large round hedge.

"Hmm. Stranger things have happened," Joe muttered. "You think this is more than just a bad year? Why these freaky things keep happening?" he continued, above the hum of the trimmer. "Plagues, Joe, one after the other. See that hurricane that just came up the coast last month? Now, they're tracking another one. These storms rarely ever come up this far. We had two in a little over two months."

"I don't want to have no dealings with wasps, those things swell me up all over. I'll take a hurricane any day." B paused to look at his handiwork. He sneezed, turning around to look at his friend.

"B, man you ever wear that mask when you go out?"

"Mask, hmm, the wide tight one," he sported his trademark half-grin, "it's somewhere in the house under the cushion, in some corner of the couch, probably."

"I'm gon' get Mel on your case. This virus is no joke. It's mutating, you know. She'll rail into you."

"Hmm, this damn thing on my face all the time is too much, man."

"She means well, keeps you living. The next time I see you go out without it, I'll tell her."

"Don't worry. She'll stuff the tight disposable ones in my pockets, those shiny blue ones that the strings cut off the back of my ears, no getting around it."

The piercing sound of sirens blasted through the air, silencing both men and forcing their heads in the direction of the sound. The lights circled atop the emergency vehicle that had come to a sudden halt at a house on the far end of the next block. Two men exited the van, quickly climbed the stairs without ringing the bell and walked into an open door.

"I wonder if it's Mrs. Rushing's grandson? You know he lives there by himself now?"

B silenced his trimmer and laid it on the path next to the fence as Joe walked down the steps. They both inched toward the sidewalk for a clearer view.

"After she passed away last March, I haven't seen much of him. Don't know who else lives there now. It's always been quiet, but you never know with young folk. I thought he moved or was away, in college or something, real smart kid."

A stretcher was being lifted up the stairs and into the home. Both men walked slowly towards the end of the block. By then, another neighbor came out on her porch and started looking down toward the house as well. They all stood silent for a moment, the severity of the situation punctuating the silence.

"You know he has sickle cell," Joe mentioned.

"Yeah, man he loved to eat too. I remember when he was a kid, he used to clean out the entire kitchen whenever he came to visit us. Look man, he's laid out, don't look good." B replied as the paramedics slowly came out through the front door.

They all waited in silence. The neighbor shook her head, hands on hips. The paramedics finally made their way down the steps towards the rear of the vehicle with the young man, loaded him in, and closed the door. There were no family members accompanying him, though someone appeared to have opened the door when they came in. Maybe it was his neighbor next door, a friend of his mother.

"Guess he must've called them himself. You know I can't remember the last time I saw him. B, to think of it, I haven't seen him for months."

More neighbors appeared on the next block. Suddenly, the sirens pierced through the air again. The mobile unit headed back around the corner to the local hospital just six blocks away.

"Bet it's this virus man."

"Well, this hospital is sure over capacity now with all these sick folk around here, virus or no virus." Joe muttered, "As of two days ago, my niece told me her shift was crazy. They had no room, and the bodies were being put in containers at the back of the hospital on the adjacent block."

"Really! Containers, man?" B shook his head.

"Man, life is so strange these days. We can't even leave the country. What if there is a death or an emergency at home? We're just screwed."

"The dead will bury the dead. B, they're just trying to keep people alive, but the plan is really messed up."

"You know, they called me and told me my regular doctor appointment is supposed to be done by phone now. Telesomething, the girl said."

"What the hell is this, B?"

"Yes, man. You have to see your doctor by phone. Since when I pay the doctor to 'see' my arthritis by phone?"

Both men chuckled. "Now you can do the zoom in or something online, so the grandchildren say."

"Can't imagine having to work now. Thank God we're passed that stage." Both men had worked for the city municipality for over two decades and had become dear friends. They were grateful that they could retire at a decent age, despite several periods of layoffs in the various departments and being passed over for promotions.

"You're sure right about that."

"Hell, all those evictions are happening too! Legal or not, who knows." B pointed to the only vacant two-family house on the other block.

"Yeah, you're right about that one. They told all these tenants they didn't have to pay, but now that the moratorium law is about to expire, all this rent is due. Hope they get an extension."

B picked up his trimmer again, shaking his head, but did not turn it on. "You mean to tell me a rich country like this, boasting all this strength, can't help their people in times of crisis? Little countries are doing much better than ours."

"This bug done overtook this place. Sure brings this place to its knees."

"And bars are still open, and I hear in some parts of the country, planned festivals going on too. When this thing slaps us all silly, we'll learn."

Joe made it up the steps, this time to his verandah. B followed suit, the aroma from the kitchen cooking wafted through the closed windows. He pounded his stomach.

"See ya later, smells like dinner."

"OK. We'll talk later."

The sounds of sirens blared again, all headed in the direction of the hospital nearby. It was the dreaded normalcy, day and night. The bright circling lights at the end of the block were a constant reminder of more sick patients, like the flickering television screens bringing somber nightly news awaiting them after dinner. For the first time, they dreaded living in such proximity to a hospital.

CHAPTER 13

"Hey Tania, I'm sooo worried," Fabiola whispered as I entered the door for work, still groggy from a listless night. "I can't take her in. No room and the children at my place. The landlord would throw me out." She waved her hands in a shooing fashion, her brows furrowed and her accent more pronounced. It was a conversation we started over a week ago at her last visit. She was frantic and resumed our last conversation without as much of a hello.

"How many children did you say your sister had?" I asked. She lifted her right hand, spreading all five fingers.

"Oh!" I shook my head.

They're all with our brother and his family. How is she coping with all this?"

"No, no good, but grateful for a roof and food, you know." She replied, her speech halting.

"How much?" I remembered some from our last conversation, but the details were sketchy.

"Cost five hundred a month."

"What? That was for living expenses in that basement?" I blurted out way too loudly.

"She has no choice, no papers yet; they need asylum. Gangs threatened to kill the family if they stayed. And you know the kidnappings are more now," she waved her hands at the rash of kidnappings for ransom and talked about babies kidnapped in the last few months for money by the gangs.

"Yes, I heard about that. It's getting worse." I barely got a word in.

"Now, the guy did let them stay in the…the 'below' and exchange for work."

She pointed downwards to the floor in frustration, trying to remember the word.

"Basement?"

"Yeh, over six months she live there, soon they have to find new place. Things are not good with the family. The man has a sick mother, and they need the place for a new helper."

"Could she work as a caretaker for them?" I asked.

"She…um, no papers for that job," she replied slowly, trying to find the words.

I felt helpless. Here I was worried about tuition money and bills—so trivial compared to Fabiola's family's situation.

"I pray. Things are so, so bad and sometimes I try to send her money, but you know, I have my own bills to pay."

"Now schools are closed too. How are the children doing?"

She looked at the floor, silent for a time. "So many people you know they not supposed to have many people in the apartment. And study with computers, you know." Her eyes welled up.

"It's tough." I tried to console her. "At least, she can be with children now that she is with family. Babysitting is so expensive if she has to pay."

"Yes. Well, I have to finish here." Another place on the Avenue I need to do, from top to bottom." She pointed to the ceiling.

"I really hope things work out for her. Let me know if I can assist." I wondered how I could assist, I did not know anyone with affordable housing in the city.

She nodded as she gathered the cleaning supplies to continue her task. I slowly strode down the hall feeling sad and helpless, thinking of community resources I knew. Most of them were closed or understaffed due to the current situation.

"It's tough for so many people." My words felt empty, knowing that I could not directly help the situation.

CHAPTER 14

"Dear, we are in the end times. I know we are."

I turned around to see a tall woman with a wide-brimmed hat and a salt-and-pepper bun neatly tucked at the back of her head. She was dark and slim, with a stiff collared white shirt and knee-length navy skirt. We were the last two in the long social distancing line at the pharmacy. Luanne called and needed refills for both boys as I was heading back after a long list of errands and was able to get in just before closing time. She was quick to remind me about the meat and eggs in the trunk, and I reminded her that there would be a long line. The condition was out of my control, but I knew her obsession with bacteria, dairy, and meats. She claimed these medications were necessary, made them calmer, and she did not want to skip any more doses. She should have her own prescription. I dared not say that is what she was probably doing, taking a few herself.

"Just finished reading this book," the lady chimed in, breaking through my harried thoughts, "you should read it."

She handed me a copy of a thick paperback with bold, silver lettering and an orange apocalyptic cover with gray smoke and lava pouring out of a mountaintop. Lightning bolts extend to the edges of the paperback. From six feet apart, I turned to her and forced a smile. I might as well listen since the line ahead was rather long.

"Young lady, do you see all these happenings, all in succession?" she asked, taking a handkerchief out of her purse. Her skirt was a thick cotton material with a straight hem, making her look thinner than she really was.

"Signs, many signs and wonders," she said, loudly demanding my attention.

"Lots of activity these days."

I nodded my head in agreement.

"What is your name?"

"Call me T, short for Tania."

"Nice, am Martha. Yes, the signs are all around us, but many can't see them," she continued.

"There is a season for everything. See all the hurricanes we are having this year?"

"Yes, we had quite a few, and I can't even remember their names," I replied, hoping she would relax a bit.

"We are in the midst of a plague. The media won't tell you that, dear. It's all over this world."

"Plague? Think I've heard about other plagues before."

"Yes, it is all in the Bible. This, too, must come to pass. One of the many things to come. So are the peace treaties and the tribulation. Do you pay attention to the news, dear?" her questioning continued.

"Yes, I check the news feeds." I pointed to my phone. She glanced at the screen like it reminded her of the plague she had just warned me about.

"I have a little one. Use it only when I need to call," she pointed to a large gray purse at her side.

"They are handy, ma'am. You can check the news too, you know. Also read books, and check the weather. You know we're expecting thunderstorms later tonight."

"Too many distractions in this world. The prince of the power of the air is all over the media, devouring our children's souls."

I nodded again and listened while I flipped slowly through the book she so excitedly handed me. I noticed her pulling at her mask.

She remained silent as I thumbed through the first few chapters, pausing only to look up at her a few times. She was intent on getting this information to anyone who would listen. She craned her neck as I scanned the pages. There were several references to the holy land, which she had neatly circled in pencil. I could see that she was ready for any questions I may have.

"I see lots of references to Israel. Have you been to Israel?"

"Oh, yes, years ago. It was such a joy to be there. You know, when Israel became a nation, it was the beginning of the end times."

"Well, that was some time ago. Wasn't it in the 50s?"

"It's such a short time in God's time, but we are getting very near to the end. Any time now. You also see the frequent hurricanes, the volcanos, these plagues, all the nations. That's no coincidence."

I scanned through chapter three, then four, as we moved up in line. There were references to signs in the sky, fires, and solar eclipses happening years apart. There was also a photo of some cows with a caption about rare livestock.

"Ma'am what do you know about this?" I was confused, pointing to the page with two large brown cows and wondering how they connected with the book's storyline.

She lifted her hands, her brown eyes deep, looking down into mine. As if transfixed, she adjusted her mask, moving closer, breaking the blue, circular, 6-foot distancing marker on the floor. I politely looked down at the blue orb, then back at her. She paused, shook her head, and stepped back to her circle.

"These rules won't save us. See, we don't have a cure. Look at all the variants. And no one is listening. All of this confusion around us is from the Devil. Our God is a God of order. The current lack of order is not of God." In her excitement, she had forgotten my question.

I nodded again, hoping to calm her somehow. *It was good for her to vent*, I thought as I snapped a photo of the cover and quickly scanned the back cover before handing the book back to her.

I felt nervous because of the uncertainty of the future. She, on the other hand, seemed so sure.

"I'll remember the title. I could get a copy online," I assured her.

"Good, please read it. We have to get ready for his coming."

"Have you always believed in these signs?" I asked as we moved ahead another 6 feet in line.

"Yes, since I was a girl, I heard it in church. Now I preach about it. The rapture is coming, very soon."

"Rapture?"

"Yes, we will be taken up with him. Are you ready young lady?"

"Taken up? I've heard about heaven on earth and Christ coming again." I thought out loud remembering the photo of the author with a gentle stare and long beard. I wondered about the meaning of a tribulation and a thousand-year reign, but I did not want to get her any more excited. She seemed frail, and somewhat tired. I wondered what prescriptions she needed.

"We will be. If we follow God's plan."

"Thank you. Good to meet you. I'll order a copy," I reassured her again.

"God bless you young lady, be ready, keep Christ in your heart."

I headed to the pharmacy counter thinking about the possibility of peace and a new earth as the summary boasted. Seems like such a far cry from our daily living.

There are two prescriptions. Two for both boys, I remembered. I could not repeat last month's fiasco when I forgot to secure the second prescription and had to make my way back to the pharmacy. The lines were long and it was late - even the new contactless drive-through lines were a penance these days and Luanne now took to avoiding outdoors out of "fear and anxiety," as she put it.

CHAPTER 15

When the evacuation team came to transport people left in Placker Bay, a section of the city occupied by mostly Black families who had lost value in their sole properties decades ago due to the construction of a shipping channel in the area, there was no excitement.

"We'll be back. It's just another one of them hurricanes." Dennis shrugged at the reporter, who was wrapping up a story on climate change and its effects on vulnerable communities.

"Yeah, I'm getting too old for this commotion," his friend Joe chimed in.

"I understand, but we gotta get out of here. Hell, I don't even have a ride and if we don't take these here buses, we gon' be stuck out here."

"I understand, son," his mother looked around at the buses lined up ahead in the large parking lot across the street while the film crew, nearby, recorded the developing scene.

"Hope it's not another major hurricane like the monster one we had. That thing damn near wiped us off the map."

She shook her head at him, looking around at the surrounding commotion.

No one took the time to determine if a full-scale operation of moving the entire city section would lead to major problems during or after the evacuation. It was another experiment by city officials, a test run for future evacuations. It was deemed necessary by the local authorities. However, the meteorologists predicted that the impending storm might not make a direct impact. The cone of uncertainty could not be ignored, not this time, the last hurricane left too many reminders.

The mayor stressed safety during his briefing the day before "to reduce the spread of the virus and protect lives," he stressed. "We need to evacuate the residents to areas of safety. Due to the rapid spread of the virus in this state, the local shelters would create an environment that could exacerbate the spread of the virus." Safety was by distance, far away, at least 60 miles. Two days before the storm, the fleet of buses was brought in to transport low-income residents. If it was anything like the last major storm, developers were already salivating.

Mrs. Williams settled into the accessible seat as an attendant strapped her into place at the front of the bus and handed her an extra mask. Her son Joe sat close by with one large backpack and tucked a small carry-on with her necessities overhead. Those who needed additional accommodations were seated before the general population.

They were at the moment graced with clear blue skies, not an inkling yet that a major hurricane was making its way up the gulf. Just maybe this time, they would be spared.

"These people are making me leave outta my place again. We don't even have a breeze over here yet. Wonder where they're gonna put us this time?" Mrs. Williams attempted a conversation with the elderly man seated across from her. His head was bowed, and his eyes remained closed as his mask hung loosely from his left ear.

"You know, they could let me die here. Lightning and rain is fine by me," shouted a feisty little woman pointing a cane as she climbed onboard, sporting a shiny silver visor and tight purple leggings.

It would be a long drive to an adjoining state, out of the hurricane's reach. Shelters were set up to house residents for the duration of the storm, a temporary stay. Police officers lined the entrance to the complex, while several volunteers did a sweep to ensure everyone who wanted to leave was accounted for. As always, there were a few who refused to leave. They were either new to the area or had somehow managed to escape the worst of the killer storm years before and were determined to tough it out again. For the first time, very few wanted to stay, the previous hurricanes had been a tough lesson.

As the buses filled up, people slowly exited the complex, passengers in a long blue and white line. This area was home for decades, generational for some, the only home they knew in this city. The lawns were, for the most part, neat and manicured, with a few overgrown lawns, some peeling paint, and a few boarded-up homes of those who never returned from the big storm.

They were headed to the interstate and for the moment, leaving the familiarity of the city. The driver tried his best to keep the passengers safe and make light of an annoying situation.

"Please be mindful of other passengers. Reminder, no smoking is allowed in this bus," he announced, "and stay tuned to the coverage for any updates on the storm and enjoy our express flight." No one laughed at the humorous attempt.

CHAPTER 16

Crowds swelled onto the sidewalks, spilling from closed storefronts, trailing down the avenue, and snaking around the corner and beyond. Protestors came from all parts of the country, some a part of organized groups. Others showed up impromptu, from social media notifications, prompted, it seemed, by a sense of national and moral duty. Some were enraged at what America had dismissed and hidden in plain sight for centuries. The callous manner of death exposed by social media of another Black man at the hands of a white police officer created a shift in focus. The officer was simply following protocol, so he thought, however brutal in this instance, supported by a system stretching back to the days of slavery. He was seen in the video with his hands on hips, boldly pressing his knee on the Black man's body—a man who cried out for help until his last breath and was ignored like an animal by all the officers on the scene. In the video, the cop who was in the process of the murder of the Black man appeared proud, as someone of his color would have been in the early 1800s at his capture of an enslaved person who had the courage to escape from the horrors of a cotton plantation.

Some labeled themselves protesting nationalists on the avenue. They consisted of some armed groups, sporting signs, some with large confederate flags. Further along, chants intermingled, some drowning out others, some calling out the current state of race relations, healthcare, housing, education, voter suppression, the environment, and other present day issues.

A group of young volunteers on the sidelines handed out water and supplies to protestors holding various signs, some too large for one person to handle. It was the third month of the protests and crowds continued to swell. This murder was filmed and on display, for the world to see. It could neither be doctored up nor drowned out by national sports, annual festivals, or firework displays. The scenes played out daily on social media and nightly news. There was no way to cover up this incident of an entitled, morally bankrupt cop, hand in pocket, callously kneeling on a defenseless Black man, taking his last breath from him on the sidewalk as bystanders pleaded for him to stop. This may have been business as usual for him, except that this time it was not.

An additional transcript was released detailing a new department cover-up in another state. Yet another white cop was predicted to get off all charges after he shot into the wrong apartment and killed another innocent Black woman. The blatant disregard culminated in a global outcry of frustration and demand for justice. As the world watched and global participation was primed, a sea of signs moved forward in unison as angry citizens carried the torches of justice.

"BLACK LIVES DO MATTER"

"SILENT NO MORE"

"DRAIN YOUR OWN SWAMP"

"WE WILL NEVER BE WIPED OUT!!" another large neon sign proclaimed.

"COLLECTIVE KARMA IS COMING FOR THIS NATION."

"ROOT THEM OUT"

"I AM A MAN 2020"

Fear of the virus did nothing to stunt the crowds. Instead, they poured into local cities including the capital, every day, some masked, others not, rain or shine. There was no end in sight.

"This is how we have to do it, whatever it takes." Melva turned to the group taking a swig from her water bottle. They drove in early, the ones who could make it, leaving at 5 am to make the 4-hour trip down for this event. I could not make it this time due to my work schedule but they posted updates along the way.

"It'll be a long one, but I am good. We've got to keep going," Jean responded.

"These people don't see they're bringing more curses upon this nation."

"Hmm, time is running out. This virus is only the start if they don't get to action," Dolan shouted.

"Right, if you think this year is bad, just wait. Each year will bring surprises. Earthquake, war. Karma."

"See, those cyberattacks were just a test run. They're trying to downplay it all."

They weaved through the crowds headed towards the large, round building at the end of the avenue. Some trees lined the sidewalks, and their lavender and purple blossoms offered beauty amidst this terse national divide. A few dark clouds loomed above in the distance, signaling possible torrential rains which were expected at this time of year.

"Four more years!" shouted a group who called themselves counter-protestors. They positioned themselves on one side of the street dressed in fatigues, following a rustic cry to their leader to save them from a society shifting and growing before their very eyes.

"No more years!" chanted an opposing group of youths inching ahead. Behind them was a group of women holding up two large printed pink banners, seemingly opposed to each other.

"Our bodies, not your rights." and "Every Life Counts."

You see some of these groups here?" Yohan questioned. "They're here with their own agenda, trying to capitalize on the real message of this protest."

"You read my mind," Melva replied.

"Like being overrun by everything else. What's new in this country?" shouted Jean tripping over a broken sign underfoot. "Guess we'll see in the weeks ahead."

"Look." Melva pointed to the broken sign at Jean's feet.

"Immigrants Matter Too."

The curfew would be reinforced as it had for several nights, only to be broken by frustrated citizens. The night prior, two people were fatally shot by someone, a private citizen, claiming to be assisting with law, and order. The self-proclaimed protector was seen brandishing an automatic weapon in the streets during the protest without any restrictions from police at the scene. A verbal altercation escalated to violence. There were numerous officers on location. However, none chose to police this individual that fateful night. A group of drumming protestors drowned out the sounds. Many in the vicinity missed the initial confrontation between the two groups. When the shots were fired, it was too late.

CHAPTER 17

I pulled a handful of clothes out of the dryer, tossed them into the large wicker basket, and carried it into the nearby room. They were still warm. I grabbed a little shirt, tucked in each side, and both sleeves, ignoring the new folding gadget Luanne begged me to use on the table nearby. This was a quick and perfunctory task, and reminded me of my mother, who, decades ago, came to this country and took care of privileged kids. She took pride in folding, feeding, wiping, and nurturing them. Laundry was not my specialty. She later told me some were sad years, especially when she missed us, her family, culture, and country. The opportunity came only once. She had to make that choice, and would remind me in a firm way.

"Mom, I want my friends to come over." I heard the boys hounding their mother again.

"Please?" they begged, for the third time, one following the other into the adjoining study nearby.

"Sorry, boys, but remember, we all just can't get together now. There is an uptick in the virus, and we have to stay quarantined for another week. OK!"

I heard a groan and could almost see their frowns and shoulders slumped while looking wide-eyed at her. She pleaded, as though they were supposed to grasp the clinical concepts of this pandemic, and they had been through it before. They marched off to the playroom. All was still for the moment as I continued the task at hand.

Luanne's voice carried from the study, high-pitched with a giggle every now and then. She was in the process of expanding an online stay-at-home podcast with a few friends. The conversation was well underway when the boys came in. It was perfect timing to illustrate her current plight. They were loud, and I got wind of their frustrations as the group continued to rant. I could hear one intermittently whining about stress. The door was open, so I had to distract and quiet the boys somehow and keep them from further interrupting the session in progress. My folding was furious now as I made my way halfway through the pile of small articles, jeans, and cotton jerseys.

"I just can't deal with the girls underfoot every day, they just can't seem to get along of late. And it looks like Sarah's hair is falling out." It sounded to me like Kate was on her usual soapbox.

"Oh, no! Well, I have no idea what to do with their algebra. You remember the first few days, the connectivity was terrible. Everything has been so unorganized."

"I know, wasn't that terrible? And there are some kids who don't even have reliable internet access in rural areas. How sad." Luanne chimed in.

"Sad to you, but you wouldn't even begin to understand," I mumbled, taking a handful of folded clothing down the hall to the bedroom dresser, the blue one shaped like a boat. As I walked down the hallway, I leaned over to shut the door to her makeshift office, but Luanne saw me and feverishly motioned, beckoning with both hands, eyes wide, an open laptop on her desk.

"Guyyys, I want you to meet my savior!" she shouted into the screen. "She's great with the boys. I don't know what I would do without her. She's filling in for DD, just for a while. You know she is in school and all and came up here with us. Even missed her group trip for us." I froze, too late for the silent, hard *no* that had formed on my lips.

"We'd love to meet her," I heard as I walked towards the desk, resting the armful of clothing on a nearby chair.

"Hi, everyone." I pasted on a smile, peering into the screen. They responded in kind, with wide well-planted grins.

I recognized three of the seven faces right away from their squares on the screen. Her best friend Liz, Rebecca and another shopping buddy next to Kate.

"Welcome, we'd love to hear how you're coping with all of this," Liz chimed in, her hair thin, spiked, and a bold red.

Luanne cajoled me into her chair, standing over me. An awkward silence followed as I stared at these women with whom I was convinced I had no shared experiences at any time in my budding years on this planet. I had to say something.

"Well, the schedule change is hard. My assignments are mounting, and classes are no longer on schedule." And I wanted to add *worse yet, I'm stuck up here in this strange place in this fiasco* but I couldn't.

"Crazy, right? Are you able to see family and friends? Oh! By the way, I'm Gina," responded an unfamiliar face on the bottom center square.

"Not much at all." I responded." It's hard, can't go out. The restaurants are closed when I go into the city."

"I know," she replied, reaching to her right for a wine glass. "There is always liquid therapy. Ask Luanne!" Her high-pitched laugh followed. "Red, brown, yellow, pick your color?" she quipped.

"She doesn't like that kind of therapy, I always offer," Luanne responded, shifting a large mug with pens at the end of her desk.

I felt a lump in my throat. *How could I stay in this chilly room with a screenful of women, with wide windows, a cloudy sky and an armful of laundry nearby? How is this therapeutic? And eerily silent now. Where are the boys anyway?*

"Well honey, bless your heart, I'm sooo sorry. I feel the same way," another woman with a southern accent crooned into the screen. "Can't travel. I can't even go to the nursing home to visit my mother; the kids really miss their mee-maw. We won't go for fear of spreading this virus, so sad. My brother has it, you know. I'm Rachel, by the way. So nice to meet you."

"How is he doing?" I asked.

"Donny still has major problems. Bless his heart. Even after a month in the hospital, he's as limp as a dishrag. Still has pain in his chest, a terrible headache, is out of breath, and told me he can't remember nothin'. Brain fog, they call it."

"Sorry to hear about it."

Mrs. Moderator was at my side, leaned in and seemed to be genuinely concerned about others, a rare thing to behold.

"I heard about this brain fog and weakness lasting long afterward," she responded.

"Yes, Luanne, my baby brother was full of life, always on his boat. He loved fishing. Now it's hard for him to get out of bed. Sometimes, I have to beg him to talk to me for two minutes. Not like him. He said he doesn't even have strength some days to go to the damn bathroom," Rachael replied.

"You know, my sister downstate said that she is so exhausted from these extended shifts, and the hospital is so crowded and understaffed. They've been requesting lots of overtime from them. Nurses are leaving in droves, traveling for more pay, I hear. Now she can't work extra shifts anymore because mom can't make it with her kids," Liz blurted out, tears in her eyes.

I heard the boys bickering again, heading back this way.

"Thanks for listening. I hope things get better…" I looked at Luanne and pointed to the door in the direction of the noise. I got up waving, relieved to be out of that room.

"OK, thank you for sharing with us and come again," Liz replied as I got up and Luanne scooted back into her chair.

"She's great with the boys," she repeated. "Well, that is our new normal," she continued as I headed towards the row in progress and wondered when and if there would ever be a normal again.

CHAPTER 18

"You know what that man did? It's unconscionable. Melva removed the lid from the boiling pot with a towel, putting it to the side as she stirred vigorously with her other hand.

"No, I have not seen any news today. Sometimes it's too much for me. Every day it's more trauma, bad on top of worse," Ann shouted as she walked around the center island towards the pot on the stove. "It's always something extra, something crazy." Letting her nose guide her, she added, "This smells sooo good."

The restaurant was temporarily closed due to social distancing rules, so they took turns meeting at each other's homes. Will announced on the last night they met that their favorite spot would be closed due to the stay-at-home guidelines. He had no choice but to let his staff go without pay and was worried about them. He even offered to help with some expenses if they were in dire need.

"To know about this disease, the spread, and not get on the ball with it at the onset! There is no excuse in a country with these many resources."

Melva paused to taste the soup, sprinkled a little salt from her orange shaker, placed the lid back on, and turned the heat down to a simmer. She opened the drawer nearby to remove the spoons for the soup. She then walked around the counter and removed several large green floral bowls and matching plates.

"Yes, it's all over the news. The death toll was rising, and in the meantime, many people— including you-know-who— in this country, were in denial. They carried on like it was no big deal and blamed the virus on another country. Like that was going to make it all disappear." She stirred vigorously, a frown on her forehead and placed the large wooden spoon down with force, flinging some of the thick soup onto the countertop.

"Oh, damn it." She pulled a paper towel from the roll nearby to clean up the mess.

"Are you surprised?" Jean responded, her forehead wrinkled. "Who blames the virus on another country while ignoring the spread in your country? Did not 'go away' as they said it would."

"Well, you think he'd know it would hurt him in this election season. Fooolish! His followers are now left in disbelief with their pants down and not enough votes. They are scheming now to get fake votes, recounting for the umpteenth time and trying to bamboozle the people."

"Sometimes I just get sick of this place."

"Well, you know what SOMEBODY would tell you?" June grumbled.

"What?"

"Go back to where you came from, that blankity blank country."

"You're right, Ann," Eva chuckled.

"And don't even try to climb back over these majestic, stunning walls and borders for reentry anytime soon!" Eva continued in a deep, pompous tone, eliciting a resounding cackle from the group.

"Like they own the world and everyone in it. Can't even begin to govern their own minds, much less a country." Melva said, removing a hot loaf of bread from the oven and placing it on a cooling rack.

"OK! I think it's about ready. It's been all afternoon; should be just right. The bowls are over there. Help yourselves. She placed a brick of butter nearby, pulled a bread knife out of the drawer and smiled at the group.

"Smells divine, and that bread looks good," Jean responded, the first to grab the ladle.

They sat down with large bowls of yellow split peas soup filled with plantains, potatoes, carrots, and dumplings with chunks of beef and extra bones left in for flavor. The TV mounted on the wall was spewing angst. B was out with his friends tonight missing out on his developing news. He seemed to make himself scarce when there was a meeting at home these days.

There was new evidence in another breaking story, of the rising death tolls, way over two hundred thousand now. Apparently, new side effects that last for months, with no relief on the horizon. There was a promise of new vaccines, but that was not yet implemented and seemed more like a dream than soon to be reality. The blogs and memes spewed dark humor of orange wigs and bleach, wipes and spray, sanitizer spoofs, quarantine quartets, and sharp dance moves, all posted daily, in attempts to ease the cloud of global anxiety and grief.

"Could you imagine the transition now? Who knows. All these people will come out in the streets for one-issue-or-another!" Jean pontificated, slowly sipping her soup.

"Ummm…This is delicious. Just like mama used to make it." She continued and these ignoramuses just don't know what the outcome would be for them."

"I want my old president back," Melva stated as she took her seat at the table. And that, they all agreed upon.

The comfort food was perfectly filling as the fallout of the current events was debated late into the evening. The conversation wafted through the kitchen for hours, along with the savory smell of delicious soup.

CHAPTER 19

Victims of the worst wildfires to hit the southwest in over a decade were stuck in long lines on the main highway. A few disabled vehicles were pushed off the highways by fellow travelers to the shoulder, plum out of gas. There were dozens of casualties, and the numbers were sure to climb as rescuers went door-to-door looking for anyone left in the area. Dozens of homes and businesses had already burned, and the latest news footage showed a gray, bare background and a frantic mayor begging residents to take heed before it was too late. There were reports of people barely escaping in time due to the speed of the winds in the area.

Firefighters were being brought in from nearby states to help in yet another national disaster.

"My cousin lives out there," Melva complained, "and I don't think I can reach her."

"I really never liked that part of the country. I visited a few times but just was not taken with it. Uncle B mused. "How are they gonna get all these blazes under control? There is no way with those earlier fires still not put out. Look at that." He pointed at a wall of smoke and orange flames. Maybe they need more controlled burns or something. Out of this world."

"No time for that. They're too busy putting out fires every week. Nowhere is safe now. Hurricanes all over the place, fires, political unrest, all at the same time." Melva stared at the screen, shaking her head.

"Well, I bet those locusts are coming next. God is trying to tell us something."

"B, you might be right," she chuckled, "you're always saying something contrary, but I may have to agree with you this time."

"It's not contrary, dear. Don't you see it happening? What else do we have to witness to pay attention? Meteorites? Nukes?"

Melva suddenly got up from the couch and headed to the kitchen, leaving B glued to the TV. He was always conscious of current events, which fueled their daily discussions, but these past few months were overkill.

Enough bad news for one day, she was not about to stew in it. She couldn't muster up another apocalyptic scenario in her head tonight; there was enough already this whole week.

"You need anything?" she shouted from the refrigerator.

"Bring me a beer! And a pack of crackers if you love me."

"K."

He started talking to the screen as soon as she left. Then he flipped again to the special on the American food insecurity problem.

He would keep flipping channels, the remote glued to his right hand and pointer finger. Melva couldn't take the constant stream of bad news, not tonight. Better turn in early.

"Why does this woman keep saying food insecurity? Just say people hungry. Pot and belly empty!" He complained as she handed him the beer. He was now irate. His accent was punctuated, and his head was loaded with memories of childhood when food was really scarce. Bush tea with a handful of crackers was the savior of his family many nights, too many to count.

"Well, B, in this country, they got to have a fancy term for everything," she replied, handing him a bowl of pretzels. Melva could hear the grandkids in the basement amusing themselves. Being grandma was a comfort- much-needed comfort. Back in the kitchen, she opened the microwave, removed the plastic wrapper from a bag of popcorn, placed the first bag in the microwave, pushed the button, and repeated the process two more times. She felt drained as she headed down the stairs to the noisy basement with two large bowls in hand.

"Thanks, grandma." The kids chimed as they grabbed a handful of popcorn each.

"Too much noise, don't get your grandpa annoyed. He'll send you all to bed in a hurry. And take those pillows off the floor."

"Yes, ma."

"No drinks down here, don't need to clean up sticky goo."

With that, she walked back up the stairs, too tired to marinate the meat for tomorrow's stew. She handed B his bowl of popcorn and crackers.

"Thanks dear. Some salt?"

"You know you don't need any more salt. Those crackers you have are salted, so is the popcorn and enough butter already, so don't ask. I'm bone-tired."

He nodded silently, waiting for a masking lecture to compliment the dietary one. It never came.

"Well, I'm gonna watch the rest of this," he replied. "Coming up soon."

Melva headed up for a hot shower and welcomed the stillness upstairs.

Wet, overcast, glad I don't have to leave the house this morning. The sun's hiding. Wonder how she's doing. Haven't been to church in so long, maybe I should start back when the mandates are lifted, but I still feel disconnected. People are friendly, but it doesn't feel like before. Everything's changed—remote services now. If you chose, you could view remotely at 10:00 am on Sundays. One lady caught the virus, came to church on a Sunday and died within three days of the visit. Made the older parishioners scared. Then the rules changed. They were mad about the regulations against indoor gatherings, and they could not attend church anymore. Mad since people were partying on beaches in large numbers in other states. That probably meant more burials in those areas.

Well, Luanne I dreaded calling her. These people live in la la land. She had to postpone her cruise, wanted a refund, and had me on the phone recently holding for umpteen minutes. When they finally got on, I had to have them call her back. They were asking for reservation numbers and stuff that I didn't have. She went off when they offered her a future trip instead with more perks. You'd think that she was given only two days to live the way she shouted at that poor guy over the phone. She rattles my nerves. Poor Bill, I feel sorry for him.

I don't know if I can do that degree anymore. Everything is complicated now. Virtual courses, no set schedule. As my aunt says, "money doesn't grow on trees." Money is tight, and I have the concentration span of a bee. Like I was asymptomatic, caught the virus, and got brain fog. My family wouldn't understand, but it's my money and my life anyway. I just need a pet right about now, like the cat I had when I was little.

CHAPTER 20

At approximately ten in the morning last Monday, social media blew up with the breaking story of a raid on a compound hidden away in the woods, in a small town, somewhere in the middle of the country, close to the Wolf Run River. Ten men were found huddled in a large cabin in a heavily wooded area with underground storage and taken into custody. They reportedly tried to carry out a foiled plot to capture the mayor and his family and take them to the mountains. There were materials in their underground location for bomb-making, rounds of ammunition, food supplies, and several copies of an incredulous manifesto outlining their goals and lofty far-reaching plans for the entire country.

"We must take them out, too many radicals. Our commander warned us years ago to protect our country. We have to grab the reins before it is too late," one of the men with a long brown beard and wide eyes shouted at the cameras as he was being led away.

"Where did they get these people? What area is this anyway?" Luanne shook her head, pulling her blond tresses into a ponytail while staring at the TV on the far wall. I was not at all surprised.

"Does it matter where? This is ridiculous, a new low. They get stranger every time, further down the hole they go." Bill muttered, staring at his computer screen, "A country full of bozos. I swear these people are alien offspring from an alternate universe."

For once, Luanne did not contradict him. She continued chopping tomatoes and adding olives to the large bowl sitting on the thick black and white marble counter. I looked at her hands. They were shaking. She put the knife down and tried to twist the lid from a jar of artichokes and could not muster the strength. She walked over to Bill with a deep frown and handed him the jar. The boys opted out of the salad as they looked at the artichokes and crumbled cheese their mom added to the bowl. She shook her head and sighed.

"I just don't get it…" she trailed, walking towards the sink as if too stressed to complete the impending task. She ran warm water over her hands, made a dab at the nearby towel, and suddenly headed across the room to the dark leather sofa to lay down, placing both her hands over her face. Bill headed over in her direction to perform his perfunctory comforting duties. I got the salad dressing and reached for glasses and plates. I knew this scenario too well, and the kids were hungry.

"I need some tea." She muttered as she laid on her back, massaging her temples with one foot off the sofa. There was half a cucumber left on the counter. I reached for the box of chamomile tea and wrapped the cucumber before placing it in the freezer. It would most likely be a part of her beauty regimen in the morning, the one which she said kept her mother looking young well into her seventies. Bill left the room and returned quickly with a warm washcloth which she plopped onto her forehead. I placed her favorite mug and jar of honey next to the box of tea for Bill to make it just the way she liked it.

"How do you make bombs anyway?" Alex asked, a frown on his face, typing into his phone.

"You'll have to get the tutorial directly from these Bozos," Bill responded, looking down at his son.

"Stupid, just asinine. All of this. And this never-ending virus. What next?" Luanne responded from the depths of the couch. "You don't just kidnap people and threaten to blow them up because you have a different worldview. We vilify people from other cultures but want to do the same violent stuff over here."

"Supposedly, the manifesto specified that they were protecting the sovereignty and true history of the nation dear," Bill droned, his sarcasm piercing.

I remained silent. I could not make light of this. Best not to get into that conversation at all. Guess people did not get the memos of the ravages of the prior World Wars and were doomed to repeat history.

"But dad, how do you protect people by blowing them up?" Alex asked, confused. The usually quiet kid was inquisitive tonight.

"Not possible, son. Not possible. Salad is ready. Pizza still hot."

Last week it was a case of congress to get Luanne to agree with contactless pizza delivery since she tried to make them at home 'from scratch and virus free,' she explained. Her attempt failed after she burned her right pinkie on the pizza pan. The half-cooked dough and veggies ended up in the garbage disposal, and she did not make another attempt. The next day, Luanne relented. The boys leaped from their stations and headed towards the boxes; they jumped for joy when pizzas were delivered and left on the front porch as Luanne instructed. I handed them plates with a little salad on the side. They did not object this time, but it was an afterthought with their focus on the thick slices of pie.

"Dressing?"

They were too intent on pulling and devouring the pepperoni to care. Bill walked dutifully to the couch to bring Luanne her tea.

"What would you like, dear?"

"Just some salad with lite vinaigrette."

I prepared a bowl and handed it to Bill as he walked back to the kitchen. Silence was best. The boys were swallowing the last of their first slice, soon to return for a second and then a third helping.

"Drinks, anyone?" Silence again.

I sat down to two slices of chicken and spinach, with a large bowl of salad and tried to tune out the entire evening.

Luanne got up, red in the face and made her way to the kitchen without touching her salad.

"Good! I want some more," Josh said, climbing off his chair.

"Me too," Alex followed, his mouth full, with half a slice still left on his plate.

"Help yourselves," I pointed to another box nearby.

"These are some big slices," he crooned.

"You have a bottomless stomach," she pointed to Josh's stomach.

The room fell back into silence; after all, this might be my last slice if we were going to get blown up anyway. Who knew how far this paranoid underground network had spread. We will have to see the latest developments tomorrow, especially the kidnapping details.

CHAPTER 21

There were more arrests the following afternoon. Ten group members lived in the vicinity of the compound and were rounded up at the time of the initial arrest. Four other men who were part of the network were also detained. The last one was captured in the basement of his parent's home a few miles away. He was led out in handcuffs, looking defiant and cursing at the officers. He claimed to be a veteran, but no records were found confirming his patriotic duties.

Two women were also taken into custody for questioning. One had an infant wrapped unceremoniously in a brown blanket. The child, presumably hers, was taken by a relative before she was led away from the premises. Most were living off the grid and reportedly had been planning this stint for months.

"Could you explain the reason for living out here, so far from town?" asked the novice reporter as a young man with the T-shirt covering his head was being led away. One of his shirt sleeves stuck up, like an elephant's ear, close to the microphone. He must have had some difficulty fumbling with the shirt and covering his face before he was led out.

"It's freedom, man. It's what we'll fight and die for in this country!" He sounded muffled, defiant.

"How long have you lived out here?" The reporter looked bewildered.

"Long time, two years now."

The woman who had to leave the infant followed in tow. As she reached the reporter, she shouted into the mic, "We must put a stop to all these rules! It's corrupting our country, the purity of it, how we want it. We must defend our rights. Young man, we all are losing our freedom, language, and our children too, to these far-leaning folks and these immigrants who are changing our language and heritage."

"Can you explain what you mean?"

"They want to change our history. They want to teach things to our children that are not *our* history, that is against our agenda, against us, the rightful people, and make our children feel bad about themselves."

"Why would you fight against a history that explains all of the facts of this America?"

"We have our facts. We should continue to write our kind of history, young man."

She scowled as she was led into the vehicle. They headed into a sea of agents and were loaded in, leaving the cocoon of tall pines and solitude in exchange for circling lights that would take them away in separate vehicles. The cabin seemed oddly misplaced in the wash of lush green, the tall pines in the background. This dirt road had lost its privacy, the solace forever changed.

A larger grid of faces was on display that night as details unfolded. They ranged from ages 23 to 55, all white males. The two women seen earlier were not on the grid. There were reports of possibly other affiliated groups from the same area and a growing concern about their online presence and influence across the nation.

"That's what we want. Our history as we know it to be, our land as it was and should be, our laws, our nation, for us, the rightful ones! We are entitled to it." The agitated man with the red cap shouted, pointing at reporters, his left hand adjusting his cap.

"We, as members of The Pure United Federated Front, stand ready to defend our land, our rights, and our freedoms," shouted an older member, the apparent leader, stunning the reporter. His bravado was evident as he looked around, seeking applause. There was none.

"With the current quarantine, polarity in government, and lack of employment, it's the perfect storm for online recruitment by these fringe groups. A special report on their efforts to penetrate further into mainstream media is coming on Friday night at 8 p.m." The station flipped to a commercial break.

More semi-automatic stockpiles were recovered in this rifle-friendly state, where the gun laws were lax, and most people welcomed it. As the plot details unfolded, there were secret weekly drills rehearsed, meetings, and trips to the mayor's home in preparation for the foiled capture. *Defend our land, stand our ground, defend our children* was the motto of this group headlining the evening news. There were some veterans included in the group but mostly younger civilians, seemingly confused and seeking purpose. Some had prior military training abroad. Photos of their stockpiles of food and ammunition were in evidence. There would certainly be more to come.

I knew they were coming. No surprise. A red sunset lay ahead as we sped through the never-ending stretch of road with tree-lined forests on either side. There were no signs of a rest stop, gas station or a small town in sight. They came into focus suddenly, stationed on both sides of the streets, guns pointing, some of the men with flags covering their faces. Several large dogs were held back at their feet, ferociously barking at the cars speeding by. I could not remember the name of the large bushy breed. No one stepped into the road as we sped by, windows rolled up. It seemed like they were yelling profanities, but with the windows rolled up, we couldn't hear.

The red ball was almost gone now, the sky a soft gray. Still miles away from a hotel. My heart was thumping. Instead, another band of soldiers lined the streets ahead, their green tankers parked, taking up one lane of the highway. I had never seen these uniforms, a dark green with thin stripes. They advanced slowly and deliberately toward the truck in front of us. The driver slowed down, forcing us to do the same. I looked back over my shoulder, confused. A helicopter blared above, thundering. We were stuck in this mire. Whom were they defending? Not us. Shots rang out.

I sat up, gasping in the dark, my heart pounding. The covers were practically on the floor. I reached out, feeling for the side table and could not find my glasses. I headed to the bathroom, one foot cold, missing a sock, and clinging to my robe.

CHAPTER 22

Briars Cove Residential tried to keep up with the new guidelines. The long list of rules was growing by the day, per CDC guidelines. The administrator punctuated her weekly online briefings with all the recommendations and reasons why we could not visit our relatives as a family.

In late spring, there were alarm bells of death clusters at nursing homes nationwide, at least four homes with over one hundred elderly resident deaths in a relatively short period. No visitors were allowed there. Not even in their last moments of life, family members could not enter the premises to visit residents. Since the mayor was blamed for the initial spread, these facilities remained in lockdown, and recovering patients were not allowed to visit with family as before.

"Here she is," the nurse said as Mrs. Pauletta's face came into view. She looked thinner than the last time I saw her and was propped up on pillows today. I adjusted the laptop, remembering her years ago as a vibrant member of her community. She was friendly and loud, someone I could not forget and I made time to keep up with her when I could.

"How are you Missy?" her voice was still strong, her tone deep.

"Good to see you. How are you feeling?" I smiled, mortified by the bone-colored blank wall behind.

"And where is your boyfriend?" I joked, hoping to make her cheer up.

"Oh, these fools took him and put him in another wing."

"And where are your pictures?"

"Boxed away too. To disinfect, they say, too much clutter. Girl, it's been too long. I need my damn pictures and the ones with my chickens are gone." She complained about those old pictures taken in her backyard, years ago right after she retired.

"We had to quarantine those infected and sanitize the entire wing yesterday," the nurse chimed in behind her, forcing a tired smile.

"Oh? How bad is it?" I asked, dreading the response. She cautiously looked around, then back at the screen.

"The curve has been flattening the last two weeks, but our precautionary measures are still to continue the protocol until there is a ninety-five percent decline from the peak."

"It's bad. I haven't seen Al, they are not bringing me to see him," she glared at the nurse.

"It's OK. You'll see him real soon, Mrs. P."

I looked at the screen, pointing my fingers at her, hoping she would stop being a pain.

"Where is my letter? And my photo? You promised to send me a framed one, remember?"

"Oh, you did not get it yet?" I asked the nurse. It was strange communicating with her on screen.

"We have to hold all incoming mail. It'll be a while."

"Could you give me the stats?" I nodded, feigning agreement, but it was all too alarming.

"Sorry, I'll have to transfer you to administration for these details."

"I understand. You're not allowed to say."

I'll have to find out later. I had another source, a mouthy insider source.

"Won't even deliver the mail on time. I can't go out to see the peacocks. I only see them when they pass by my window," Mrs. P complained loudly.

"We all have to follow rules these days. I can't go out due to the curfew. Just about everything I do is closed, even the gym, and I have to wear a mask too." I pointed to my nose, poking it, hoping to get a laugh.

"You don't need to be going out at night anyways. The mask keeps the boys away," she cackled again.

"Well, you're looking good. Hope your man will get better."

"Yeah, I'm worried. Need to get my hair done. See what mess they have it in, if you call that combing." I nodded at her, trying to keep a straight face.

"It looks OK, wish I could come braid it for you. We only have a minute left, wish I could come see you."

She groaned. I lifted my arms around to give her a virtual hug. Her friend was in quarantine, and as I got ready to sign out, I had a sinking feeling that I might not get to see him alive again.

I could see the exhaustion on the attendant's face when she came into the room and around the side of her bed. They had to be short-staffed and burned out.

"Thank you so much for the chat. I'll contact the administration later." I forced a smile at the nurse, ignoring the knot in my throat.

"You're more than welcome, have a good day."

She waved at me.

"Bye, come see me soon."

Looks like Mrs. P was well on her way to becoming a techie. She just might send me a selfie one of these days.

I knew whom to call. One of the cooks at the facility lived down the street and knew Mrs. P. He could give me details. The administrator's job was to make the place out to be the safest in the city, but I knew better. Her hands were tied to her paycheck, and jobs were now so few. A discussion with this administrator would be a waste of time.

CHAPTER 23

The candidates flew around the battleground states with election day swiftly approaching. Pundits debated the results ahead of time, each side staking the possibility of a win. Statisticians rolled their skewed dice to either end of the spectrum while political fundraisers pleaded their causes and shoveled vast sums into their pots of choice. So much money was raised that the sums of both parties combined could easily fend off world hunger for years. Along party lines, citizens provided unconditional support for their candidates, even if out of touch with reality, proudly strutting their respective colors and slogans on their foreheads and chests.

The latest viral hiccups exposed hilarious logistical flaws in this feverish electoral process which would intensify until election day. Memes riddled with sarcasm exploded one morning, revealing a half-empty venue for one candidate who boasted about a packed-to-capacity event. A large crowd waited patiently in frigid temperatures for buses to transport them to the main venue for a rally, only to be left stranded and frostbitten. Late into the frigid night, the wait continued, until the frostbitten received transport to the emergency room by ambulance instead of the promised bus ride to the now-infamous rally.

Lines wrapped around buildings as the doors opened on voting day. Early voting numbers were staggering. As we stood in line, I could only hope that the drama would subside. But this year looked like it could easily roll into the next, like a half-filled barrel tumbling sideways down a hill in no clear direction. It was nerve-racking standing out here with news of a new viral strain on the way.

The rate of reinfection was alarming. No one expected to hear that there were at least two current strains, one more infectious than the other. With a vaccine now ready for distribution, frantic statesmen and women huddled among themselves to devise a distribution plan. One state realized the bumble of logistical errors after choosing a first come, first serve plan for the vaccine. In one case, lines were wrapped around the convention center the night before as a few young people camped out with gray wigs and other ready-made disguises to get ahead of the line. As a result, that state ran out of doses before seniors who needed it most could get their vaccines.

The line inched forward at a steady pace. *Another half hour, this should be over. I've never seen such a large turnout.*

I kept my eyes glued to my phone, eavesdropping to kill time. Two women were having an animated conversation about all things current.

"I'm not taking that damn shot," shouted a petite lady ahead in line.

"Meee neeether." The lady directly in front of me responded to her friend before turning to look back in my direction. I ignored her. She rubber-necked back, realizing that I may not be a great candidate for her conversation.

"Don't know what they got in that thing. Have you ever heard of a vaccine created so fast?"

"Never."

"You heard about the strange side effects, like palsies? Yeah, your face lit-er-ally falls on one side. Brain fog, who wants that?"

"Better not try to make me vaccinate my children. Heard it might affect working people if they choose what to put in their bodies? How crazy?"

They were both maskless, like a third the people waiting in line. It was the national bone of contention, that along with the notions of unfair election practices. The loud motor of a bike disturbed my eavesdropping, and I looked across the road to see a large sign on the pharmacy front nearby, "Get your flu shot today." *I already took mine—one less thing to worry about.* That new vaccine, I, too, was unsure about, but I would rather gamble with life and a side effect than a ventilator and possibly death.

There was a large blue tarp on the building nearby, a reminder of the surprise category three hurricane that made a slow and damaging entrance over a month ago: a back-to-back surprise at that. A prior storm came and went, leaving water and a quick clean-up of brambles. The last one, however, disrupted the refineries, halting production yet again this year, and bringing a few nasty tornadoes along with it. With the hurricane seasons now getting longer, I hoped this was the last one for this misery-filled year. Climate change was a point of contention in this election. These were turning points that rattled so many citizens on both ends of the spectrum.

The results came in quickly, as they always had before, however, there were a few battleground states, which halted the entire proceeding. The following week, numerous lawsuits barraged the election results, but most would later be tossed out for lack of merit. It seemed like many citizens could not accept facts and instead found some comfort in hair-raising conspiracies in a country that used to boast democracy and national compromise. The inauguration went on as it always had for centuries. This time, however, many braced for a hissy fit. Still, many could not possibly accept the certified results, since they were not the ones approving this year's certification. And they could not agree to the resulting votes since the only votes that mattered were theirs. The melee culminated when a riled-up, rabid crowd who could not wrap their brains around the results pitched a fit, one that was televised around the world.

As they reeled from electoral losses, they felt it was their duty to change and remake history to suit their fancy. After all, it was a pastime in the nation to rewrite history, but it was now becoming more challenging to replicate that trick. And so, they haphazardly gathered one morning, shouted, and marched up the steps of the Main House with bats and blazoned logo hats. With hollow bravado, they scaled walls, broke glass, squeezed through windows, and injured law enforcement as they went, all while hurling insults. When finally, they forced their way into the inner sanctum, they levied excrement on the floors, ransacked offices, sat on desks, and spewed insults intent on claiming territory in a national landmark built by slaves. Days later, many were in custody, and a few were dead, including officers, following the failed attempt. The country went on with tackling the pandemic and piling on charges on many of these very rioters who sought in vain to reinstate their cult leader's lost place. We, the people, had spoken but the saga continued as many tried to face the changing realities of the nation.

CHAPTER 24

The group got together again to discuss the events that had just taken place one week ago. They exchanged ideas over another delicious fish stew in Jean's kitchen. Not surprisingly, their group was expanding with the current state of unrest. This was the night to welcome new members while planning their current and future agendas. They were also here to celebrate another birthday and Melva's recent publication.

"Remember when we went to that old neighborhood to register people to vote? No one wanted to hear from us."

"Yeah, I bet you some of them were like the people at the main gate, glad to see the chaos and shit on the floors. The gall of these people to think themselves superior, cavemen is more like it." Sherry, a new member, was still angry because her nephew worked as a security guard in the vicinity of the incident and had to be subjected to a hostile crowd and racial slurs.

"Thank God, he is OK," she said, choking up.

"The Lord we serve is sending a message to this nation. Better see the light before it's too late." She continued.

"Remember, we have diverging views on who God is, and some people think they are Gods. We may not all be serving the same God." Melva reminded them as the lively discussion continued into the evening.

After dinner, they read and discussed the recently published article in more detail. Lena read it again aloud as a reminder that solidified their purpose as a group.

"AMERICA GONE WILD"
Op-ed by Melva Mongtomery

As the world looks on in disbelief at this shameful specta-cle unfolding at the capitol in real-time, we realize that many Americans are having great difficulty coming to grips with the reality of our election results. The storming of the capital seems to be acceptable to many who are mentally incapable of accepting the verified results. This wild and brazen display proves a lack of moral and effective leadership in this country and a lack of respect for the centuries-old democratic pro-cess. Further complicating this issue, one can successfully argue that the history of the election process in this country has never been truly democratic.

When Black Lives Matter protesters peacefully marched over the slaughter of a Black citizen to bring to bear the chronic injustices riddling the nation, protestors were cat-egorized and labeled by many as criminals and thugs. Not one of those protesters swarmed and maimed security, broke windows or vandalized property in the House, and no one in that group disrespected the Floor. Who defines criminals and thugs? Well, definitions also are recrafted and remade by only a select group. Is this spectacle of middle school melt-downs acceptable simply because the results of an election were not in some citizens' favor? Is this outburst because we now have a more diverse body of citizens being sworn into this incoming administration—finally a truer representation of the U.S. population? Will these perpetrators and vandals even be prosecuted, or are they hoping for a quick slap and a pardon?

As an immigrant to this country, I realized within months of arrival that America does not belong to any one group. Native citizens will reiterate that fact if we ever need reminding. Black Americans whose African ancestors have been enslaved and forced to build the wealth this country flaunts today will reiterate that fact. Immigrants from all ends of the earth who have come to this country will reiterate that fact. So why is the obvious so complicated for some to grasp?

Like it or not, we all must truly accept this principle before the fate of our democracy can continue along an open course. Fighting this reality today is futile at best, and incredulous at worst. How can we be an example to any other country? Not until those wrangling in childhood tantrums get off the playground, take an unbiased history lesson and offer a global apology to those watching in horror in real-time.

This is a far cry from the meaning of America, and I am one of the millions of embarrassed global citizens looking on in utter disgust. The world is watching, appalled at this display of domestic terrorism, complete lack of maturity and selfish, entitled individuality. As we battle a pandemic, a peaceful transition of power should be the least of our worries. As citizens, we should face the current realities, utilize sound judgment, and rein in these wild, impetuous attitudes. As our president-elect requests, "Allow this democracy to go forward." As a nation, the time for reckless rallying and maskless partying is over. Now is high time to sober up, accept our certified election results, and work towards the semblance of a less imperfect union. May God, in whose image we are ALL created, Bless America!

I reread the article again for a third time, then plopped the phone on the charging station and headed to bed. I loved the piece. She said it well. After all, these reckless terrorists should be reprimanded for such an attack. Yes, it was an attack. There was nothing peaceful from the footage all over the news media. Officers were beaten, one killed and some experienced extensive trauma leading to suicide. For those touting law and order and protecting our men in blue, this display was complete irony and epic stupidity. But once again, the recreation of reality and the rule of law is seen here as a national pastime. Scaling walls, waving confederate flags, donning furry costumes, and pooping on the floors said it all. There were no more words. Their fears were obvious, but so were the facts.

CHAPTER 25

The vibrating buzz on the nightstand jolted me up. Half awake and annoyed, I fumbled in the dark for my phone, swiping for silence. *It must be a wrong number.* I had at least another two hours of sleep. Pulling the quilt up, I slid down, my head sinking further into the pillow. It would be a cold day ahead. I could feel it. I dreaded the trip back upstate. Bet the boys hated remote schooling with mom helicoptering them for half-day all week. This job assignment will be over soon, just a few more weeks.

The phone started vibrating again. I picked it up and pulled myself upright to look at the screen, too bright for my eyes in the darkness. I rubbed my eyes and looked again. The time registered at 4:23 am. It was Luanne. I dreaded whatever was coming on the other end.

"Hello," I mumbled.

"I just tried to reach you. Hope I did not wake you up too early."

"It's OK, I'm already up."

"So sorry." She spoke in hushed tones. *She's probably in the study at this time of the morning alone with her insomniac self. Her sleeping pills needed refilling: it was the end of the month, I knew it.* There was silence on the other end.

Luanne, is everything OK?"

"I don't want to do this, but I think it's best for us all if we quarantined as a family up here for a while. Bill and I discussed it, and since you're already in your place and we are all at home, it's best that we keep huddled, especially with the rampant spread. Well, hope you don't mind if…"

"It's OK, Luanne." I interrupted her, relieved and panicked at the same time. *Bill was not included in the "we," of course. That decision was made all by herself.*

"We would pay you, of course, for the next two weeks."

"Fine." Suddenly I wanted to sink back into bed in complete silence.

"Wish the vaccine was ready, you know. And these new strains that will come, how many?"

"Um, hmm."

I prayed for her to stop. I could not take another early morning pundit, not at four in the morning. We were all adrift, in the same boat to pandemia. What was the use of blabbering the obvious on a wintery morning? I guess, in a nutshell, I had become too much of a risk, a viral carrier, from the masses, spreading infection to the family.

"No problem, I don't mind the break. Will be in touch," I heard myself saying. "Will see you guys soon."

"I'm so sorry to wake you. Thank you for understanding." She crooned.

"Nite, Luanne."

I hung up, flustered but relieved that I did not have to go out in the cold or listen to her growing list of worries. I felt a sudden chill, dove under the quilt, and pulled the covers way up, sensing a freedom for the first time since the start of this fiasco. I chuckled, remembering last week when she greeted me at the door with a spare box of masks and two hand sanitizers 'on the house' she said, to carry with me at all times. How could I have missed that warning sign? The only problem was that I had sympathy for the family. To be locked up all day with her must be so taxing. My thoughts were racing. I offered a prayer of thanks, pulled the covers over my head, and grabbed my earbuds.

Lilting, pulsing,
steady, soothing,
closer coming,
whispering to me,
take it slow,
by the sea, la, la, la.

CHAPTER 26

At 2 pm I adjusted the laptop, relieved that it was fully charged and clicked on the link forwarded to me from the funeral home the day before. The cameras zoomed to the main entrance of the little stone church as people slowly filed past, then directly into the blue casket. The deceased lay with her eyes shut, thinner than I remembered, with a blank face. Not as lifeless, thanks to the undertaker who complimented her skin with a matching shade of brown and added some color to her cheeks. And atop her head was a light-colored hat, just the one she might have picked if she had a choice. About half a dozen family members surrounded the casket, all dressed in shades of black, navy and white. Most wore masks except one petite woman in a brown form-fitting dress, who kept walking back and forth at the foot of the casket emitting a short, sharp wail every now and then. And no one made an effort to comfort her.

The screen was buffering and froze as the woman started to wail again, turning to look at the face of the deceased lady one more time before the lid of the casket was shut. Her body was slowly carried to the front of the chapel by pallbearers, in preparation for the final mass. It was my first virtual funeral and a first for many loved ones who could not make the trip due to pandemic restrictions worldwide. The pallbearers made their way down the middle aisle to the front of the church for the beginning of the home going service, while the rest of the congregation found their seats as the pianist readied the crowd for the opening hymn.

It was a sunny day on the island, green, lush plants could be seen from the open windows. Both side doors remained open to welcome a breeze or any latecomers into the building. Several people fanned themselves on the benches filled to capacity. I grabbed a tissue nearby. The tears came at the finality of her death and the memory of the death of my mother years before, who was buried similarly in another small church a few miles away from this one.

The priest was stoic and did his best to bring some comfort in a difficult time. As I glanced to the right of my screen, I noticed there were over thirty people viewing the live stream service. The order of service continued with a reading by a nephew and the eulogy by her son.

She was a "respectable woman who dedicated her life to service," he said, "quiet, with an infectious smile, patient, especially with children. She was well known to everyone and loved by all her friends and neighbors. Her legacy spanned several generations, for she lived a long life." After the lengthy eulogy, an older man made a somber attempt at a long, mournful solo. I was grateful that he paid homage but wished there would have been an accompanying instrument, a guitar perhaps, to temper his pitch.

The second of three priests walked towards the pulpit, adjusted her wide-rimmed glasses, and gave a rousing sermon about the goodness of God and our duty to mirror a life of service, a touching homage to the deceased. I was distracted by someone walking around the back of the chapel, then heading down the middle aisle, deliberately making her way to the front. Her hands reached out to caress the top of the closed casket, and seemingly unaware of the services at hand, the lady dressed in brown burst out crying again and interrupted service by requesting out loud to view the body one more time, stretching her hands and pointing ahead towards the altar. She was comforted this time by two attendants as the final hymn was sung. After the closing hymn, she finally got her wish and she was allowed to see her aunt's face one last time. She followed closely behind the pallbearers as the casket was lifted out of the church in preparation for the burial at the adjoining cemetery. The congregants all followed the hearse to the burial site, to the grave dug six feet deep as it had been done for over a century, the red mud piled on all sides, a tradition and site I remembered as a child.

Several more hymns were sung by the gravesite in a cemetery where former congregants from several generations were buried. Two strapping young men seemed contented with the tedious task of keeping the wailing lady at a safe distance from the grave since she made her way to the edge of the pile of dirt, standing directly above the final resting place. After the priest offered a final prayer, the small choir sang "Nearer My God To Thee" as several bright colored umbrellas were unfurled. A gentle rain drizzled the crowd under a clear blue sky, as if nature itself was paying respects to the dead.

I felt the finality as the coffin was lowered and the first few piles of dirt were shoveled in with a dull thud.

"Wait! Wait, not yet!" she cried, hoping to delay the finality of the day. All three gravediggers were doing their best to finish the task at hand as large shovels of dirt were quickly tossed into the grave, unto the casket. Finally, with the last of the dirt piled in a red-high mound above ground, colorful shrubs were pushed into the dirt, then large bouquets, including lilies of several kinds, wreaths and tropical flowers, were piled above the dirt, a welcomed comfort to all looking on. As the funeral came to a close, the sun began to set, and the crowd dwindled as people made their way home. There was no more sad singing, and finally, no wailing. Though international travel was restricted for so many during this time, this live stream provided closure for many without the material boundaries of season and time zones. I was grateful to be able to pay final respects and to see my relative's face one last time.

CHAPTER 27

Downtown, the lights twinkled, wreaths sparkled, and the fragrance of spiced gingerbread cookies from a nearby bakery welcomed shoppers who came early, hoping to snag a deal before the rush of the holidays. The annual small business holiday shopping weekend was in full swing, eager to welcome anyone with a wallet. "Buy one. Get one." and "40% off" offers lined storefronts, beckoning customers to enter. The jewelry store at the end of the first block even offered cider and bubbly. Rudolph, Santa, and a traditional nativity scene dominated the small square as carols filled the air. Santa beckoned children to come and sit on his lap to give him their list for Christmas, oblivious to the long food lines across the tracks a mile away.

Around the nearby community center, cars of every make and model snaked around the building, past the park to the entrance of the local elementary school. Their occupants were waiting for the donations of boxes filled with perishable foods being handed out by volunteers in matching green sweaters, gloves, and wooly hats.

With stalled political squabbles, talk of additional government assistance was stalled for over two months. Meetings came to a halt while lines like this one grew longer across the country. "Masks Required" signs were posted at the entrance as two volunteers handed them out to those who had none. Many people arrived at the center early, hoping to beat the long lines, scared that goods or gas would run out. A few came walking, and a couple came in on a bike. Like the promise of a vaccine, these brown boxes offered hope for better things to come.

A friendly voice welcomed each car as it slowed to a halt. The occupants would roll their windows down or pop their trunks to receive the boxes of food and supplies generously handed out to anyone entering the line. Muffled "thank you's" and "God bless you's" echoed from behind masks that served a dual purpose: keeping the germs away while hiding faces filled with depression and worry.

A few defiant beneficiaries complained through the masks about the masks. In addition, they expressed their grievances about the government, and the vaccines, even as the ICU beds spilled over into hallways of the local hospitals. The governor pleaded with citizens to respect the lives of themselves and others, but refused to order a statewide mandate. Some echoed various, even colorful interpretations of "my freedom, my right," a matching response to other defiant citizens on the national nightly news. At the end of the queue, young surveyors with fingerless gloves completed a brief, optional survey at the exit, about the household size, current income, and future needs.

Those who could sneak out of the country or the major cities did so, hoping to avoid the stifling lockdowns for a more picturesque, sunny pandemic experience. Fines did not prevent the more affluent from docking their boats in the tropics, and in some cases, getting onto a few small islands. Some well-connected people escaped the worst due to experimental treatments offered to a select few.

The death toll had doubled from two weeks before, only to grow with the holiday travel. Some ignored the travel guidelines, fatigued from quarantine. They preferred to get on the move, feeling it was all too stifling to stay cooped up at the end of the year. As flights were booked to capacity, a new strain of the virus was weaving its way across the globe, with the first case traced to the West Coast. Still, the fatigue was too much to keep citizens from a brief escape, prompted by nostalgia and the welcomed Christmas cheer.

CHAPTER 28

With all of the restrictions in place, just about everyone got used to eating at home, but I missed the smells, the restaurant booths, and the banter that came along with eating out. The perfect little eatery was just a five-minute walk away. It was open with reduced hours now due to restrictions and lack of staff, like most eateries in the area. It was too early for lunch, however, I took the risk and headed down the block, pulling a brisk sprint, the best one in over two months. I prayed that the menu would be as perfect as I remembered it, with an all-day breakfast special on the menu. The "We're Open" sign blinked, ushering me in as I pushed open the red door.

There were only two tables occupied, an elderly couple in the far corner and two men chomping heartily and chatting at a table nearby. There was no one to greet me. I walked in and plopped down, as I used to before the lockdowns, and grabbed a menu from an empty table close to the entrance. I was huffing from the brisk walk. *Hmm, it is time to resurrect my scale. These pants are too tight in all the wrong places.*

I noticed the breakfast platter options were more limited than I remembered. The large omelets reminded me of late Saturday morning brunches with James after our two-hour-long gym workouts for a protein-packed breakfast. Those times seemed so long ago, yet not long enough. I felt a lump in my throat as I sat close to the side window where we would always sit; our table. I could remember the final workout and our last meal here. I still could not commit, and that would always be. He finally lost patience that day, and I couldn't blame him for feeling "strung along" as he called it. I missed him and needed company today, now amidst all of this chaos. Well, he still called, often enough, to see if I was alive. Had to give credit where it was due. When the tears came, I reached for a napkin.

"Would you like some coffee?" Startled, I looked into an unfamiliar smiling face. "Are you OK?" *She must be a new waitress. Heather her name tag read.* Keeping employees was a great feat these days, especially in the service industry. Who could blame them for wanting to avoid the possibility of being infected, yelled at and underpaid?

"Please."

She handed me a cup, and the aroma was rich. I reached for the creamer and a stirrer nearby.

"Can I have the Wednesday omelet special with everything? Extra onions and broccoli, and please, some hot sauce."

"Sure thing."

I ignored the buzz of my phone, stirred in an extra packet of sugar, and deeply inhaled the robust, rich brew as she walked away. Suddenly feeling hot, I pulled off my jacket and relaxed into the chair. It was strange to be ordering a meal mid-morning, midweek, with no kids to monitor, no assignments to complete, and no workout schedules.

The side of hash browns was divine, my very own pile of golden crispy potatoes. *So not good for me, but I love them.* I grabbed the hot sauce and sprinkled it heavily over everything. It was my first helping since the onset of the global fiasco. Heather topped up my cup and brought a glass of orange juice. The view was somewhat drab with an overcast sky, and tall brick buildings in the distance. Sirens blared from time to time. Several feet away, the two men at the next table distracted me when their casual conversation suddenly escalated.

"These cops get off every single time! "I turned around to look and my interest perked as one was Black and the other White. The White man shook his head in disbelief at yet another case on the news.

"Know what you mean, man, no justice in this place!" his friend replied, with an accent as prominent as his deep voice. His thick locks laid down his back to his waist.

"Dem riddled him up, take his last breath, after dem sit 'pon him, thirteen whole minutes!" he continued.

"Yeah. You believe this madness we continue to live in?" a third man interjected, walking past their table, a waiter leading him towards the booths in the back. He paused, before adding his piece as if he had been a part of the conversation all along.

"Happens far too damn much. Every time you check the news, it's death, harassment and murder for us Black people, and NO consequences. That made national news only because somebody filmed it and everybody was home to see it. No hush, hush secret this time. And these people like hush-hush, to breed evil." He abruptly left the table and followed in the direction of the waiter to a booth at the end of the row.

"Good thing this was exposed," his friend replied, biting into a roll.

"How you could put your knee on somebody for so damn long and ignore their cry? It's a sick, sick kinda people you hear me? Is Babylon we try to survive in. We don' belong here. They want to call dat self-defense? Is white supremacy is what you call dat, plain and simple. These folks get high off torture, sick people. This harrassment, all it does is keep their fright at bay, you hear." He pointed his finger at his friend as he continued the conversation and seemed to have forgotten the meal on his plate.

Two waiters puttered to the front, listening intently, avoiding eye contact. I looked over again at the men, my ears cocked, gulping down half of my juice. *This man was right. Plain and simple. No 'men in blue' of sound mind and basic human conscience would want any of their family members, friends or neighbors to die this way. No one should, but there are people who secretly don't give a damn or get a sick sense of satisfaction from it—upstanding folks too.*

"I agree. That was evil and stone cold murder. He shouldn't be on any damn police force, it's cowardly." His friend replied as he removed his cap to reveal a head of salt and pepper hair, thinning at the front, a match to his long beard.

"Too much infestation in dis here world, and it's comin' from the top of the pile as it has for hundreds of years. These evil mongers, tricksters, these colonizers, for centuries plotting' to rob and bamboozle the rest of the world. You cyaan'[9] get rid of our race, the original race, part and parcel of the earth no matter how hard you try. You cyaan' get rid of the salt of the earth. These fools." He pointed his index finger to the floor, then the ceiling. This action brought him back to the meal on his plate. He pulled his locks back, lifted his fork and funneled eggs into his mouth and glared over in my direction.

"True," I nodded in agreement from my table.

"We have to effect change before it's too late." His friend replied. "Bigots in uniform, bigotry on our court benches, in government."

---

9 Cannot

"Tell me, scared baldheads don't have what it takes to run a country. Power-hungry, weak-minded fools. Real men don' do that, no way."

I buttered the last of my toast, staring at my bare plate, ears glued.

"You know this is completely wrong. But you know I worked with you all these years. We're friends. I don't see color," his friend stated sternly.

Uh-oh! This is getting good.

"Black is who I am here in Babylon, I and I, the real me. Jah make no mistake when him create me. From me head to me toe, you have to see all of me. How society treats me and try to destroy me is all evil and for centuries turn upside down. You have to see it all. No color blind here in this world, if you create color in a scheme, you can' just unsee it for convenience. "

"Well…yes. I could understand your point. Never thought of it that way before." His friend put down his coffee mug, shaking his head.

"The police see color, fly into a rage and fill up wide fear when dem see me. When dem stop me, is color dem see. You hear? Doesn't make sense on Sunday in churches or any day of the week when all of a sudden dem don't see color. Bet when color walk through their neighborhood, dem see it!" His voice was deep, the restaurant, still.

"I don't have the answer, my friend, but all of this is sinful, inhumane. It's not right."

"Supremacy messes your kind up, for centuries always lookin' around to profit, to conquer everything in sight and put manmade value systems 'pon everybody, dat's the problem. Jah say to share. Your kind don wanna share. If you' trained to ignore creeds, to value and devalue by your made-up standard, you can only fix dis mess by fixing your own soul. It's all smokes and mirrors, and it'll all be dismantled, watch and see."

Sounded like the real Jesus himself was in the building. Not the floating white one perpetuated around the globe-the smokes and mirrors one.

I got up suddenly, coffee sending me to the bathroom, as it did every time. It was locked, and I motioned to the waiter nearby, he went to the back for a key. I had to wait. An odd silence hovered over the entire room.

When I returned, they were gone. I paid for the meal and headed out into the dull overcast morning, my head throbbing but with a full stomach and a wired mind. For that one thing, I could be grateful. My anxiety about work, school, travel, and responsibility for the boys was on the back burner, at least for now. I picked up the pace, pulling my jacket collar up, slowly jogging home in hopes of burning a dozen calories.

CHAPTER 29

The rumblings rose through the media for months regarding reminders of the benefits and necessities of the vaccine and the boosters. Lines were growing as the long-awaited, controversial vials promising immunity were being rolled out by major pharma. Quieter were whispers of several new strains of the same virus and the threat of spread without a promise of further immunity.

I swiped up, yet another headline, "First Responders First in Line for the Vaccine Followed by Nursing Home Residents."

I scanned my feed for something refreshing like celebrity gossip – nothing much, just the usual splits and ugly divorces.

Silly romances, 'it' couples, always the same ending.

"Blacks Vulnerable to Virus But Resist Vaccination Due to Racist History."

Well, what does this country expect? A welcoming choir?

"Broadcaster Resigned Over Comments of Major Royal Interview."

Oh, some celebrity news, finally! Him again! Must read the rest of this one.

All the major global networks covered this piece. The networks took sides, across the spectrum, this one went left. I paused, scrolling back to read this opinion piece.

In a classic case of superiority, he haphazardly walked off set, then quit because he was not allowed to foam and froth at the mouth without challenge. He'd spewed his opinions daily on air, but on this day he could not win this final argument on an issue, he clearly could not comprehend. His pride would never allow him to listen, much less apologize. These second-class news anchors should be kneeling, looking up to him for approval. Some of his colleagues and co-hosts refused to engage him and did not agree with his point of view. He stormed off live television, like a caged parrot, a victim. The very issue of victimhood he had just been criticizing this famous couple about, he mirrored himself by storming off air. After tens of thousands of complaints flooded in, he could not lower himself to possibly see that his opinion may have been flawed at least and at most offensive; his culture was based on supremacy, after all. His views were omnipotent and should always take precedence, regardless. So, he quit.

The same man, hungry for fame, who referred to a fellow team member as a servant can't see his problem. Some opinions are dangerous and unfit for global consumption, especially if stemming, in this case, from presumed rejection. Some with like minds heralded him, because secretly, they felt they should be the ones in a position of supreme power to stifle the views and conditions or any global citizen of a different creed. These sad souls could not understand that their rage also stemmed from a misguided sense of dominion, control, and entitlement to wealth, domination and connections offered, but not rightfully earned. Somehow this interview was offensive to him because the roles were reversed, and he was not in control for once. For that he was called out on live television. They would not tilt the interview in his favor, nor silence the truth coming from the segment. Not anymore.

Let me bookmark this.

For days, left and right, headlines blew up on this seemingly trite incident. The surprise was not the allegations made during the interview, but his refusal to state the obvious. He could not utter the obvious words. And for that he walked off and was let go.

CHAPTER 30

Just when some larger countries thought they had a handle on the first wave, then came a second viral tsunami. Family members in developing countries were crying to reporters on the evening news that hospitals ran out of equipment and oxygen. Family members were forced to buy cylinders and bring them to the hospital to accommodate their sick family in overcrowded rooms with bodies piling up nearby. Infected patients lucky enough to secure a bed reported lying for hours in the same room with unclaimed corpses in adjoining beds. There was a healthcare worker shortage, and some countries pushed PR damage control propaganda over the safety of citizens. There was a recent article describing erroneous identification of bodies, and coffins costing four times the usual price if you were fortunate enough to find one.

"How can we not provide for our people when we are one of the biggest manufacturers of vaccines in the world? Our vaccines are going to other countries?" A young woman somewhere overseas wept in a crowded waiting area outside of her local hospital, hoping to secure a bed for her mother." No beds, no vaccines, no oxygen, nothing."

"I hope the world can see the real story. The government doesn't want us to tell, they just want to save face," her husband joined in. The U.S. sent aid to other countries in need, and the argument continued behind pharma doors of vaccine patent restrictions and the need for international access. Big pharma already made billions of dollars in the first round of vaccines. Citizens on this side of the globe had access to several options, many pompously refusing and turning their noses up at the vaccinations in the name of personal freedom.

Another report highlighted a conscientious drug company that opted to forgo the patent-hogging traditional route. This rare gem offered a cost-effective, patent-free option for developing countries to manufacture their very own vaccines, and do so in a cost-effective way. Here was a company featured for their respect and value for humanity. Medical professionals continued to plead with the public to get the vaccines as the interest waned and fears abated. Around the country, regional newspapers refused to accept articles like this one because of local and party politics.

MASK UP AND GET VACCINATED

As a concerned citizen, I beg a simple but urgent request; please wear a mask if you are not vaccinated. A governmental mandate is not necessary. We have a choice to do what is best for the health of our communities and our country. We have had recent examples from other nations that wrestled with COVID-19 and recovered. They were inconvenienced, but they followed recommendations, practiced social distancing, and quarantined when necessary. Yes, they wore masks and were consistent with these recommendations. But once again, local and regional hospitals are close to capacity with infected patients and medical professionals are being overworked and spread thin, yet again.

The vaccine is here, there is the science and the health professionals to answer queries, and there are options available.

In other countries, only ten percent or less have been vaccinated; many of those citizens are begging their governments for assistance. Here, the vaccines are available, but many are refusing to follow guidelines in the name of personal freedom. Remember, you are a part of a larger community, even when you feel invincible or don't care how you die. Newsflash: you are not an island. Respect the lives of your fellow citizens, young, elderly, and in between. Respect the lives of healthcare workers and all others in your community, your state, and your country. We have heard for months the requests of our health officials and respected medical experts. We have seen the death tolls rise across the globe. Use common sense if you have it. Yes, you are an individual with an independent mind to choose. You are also a part of a family, a community, a state and a country. You can use this opportunity to prepare for future scenarios because there will be more. In the spirit of one nation under God, please wear a mask and take the vaccine.

Reports from the continent of Africa and other areas were sparse at best, and hard to find. Some articles voiced confusion as to the fact that the pandemic was not as ravaging in Africa and some other countries. Like a seesaw, the variants would rear their head again surely. Each surge of the virus brought a lesson in preparedness, it was up to each governmental body to learn from the results, but there was always politics in the way, and so the dead continued to pile up in places where there were not enough people or resources to accommodate the onslaught.

The variants were by no means in quarantine, they were coming and they were spreading. People longed for freedom and life as it was, with parties, barbeques, and weekend trips. Restrictions were lifted in places where the rules were relaxed, fortunately, but it was all temporary. Grief blew through the early summer air, a staunch reminder of the past year, but summer it was, and for some, the fun must go on. Cruise lines dangled endless offers to the quarantine weary, beckoning with crystal blue waters, more spacious ships, and snow-capped mountains. However, in many industries, employees were sometimes hard to find. Many quit altogether while others opted to stay home permanently.

A third vaccine booster was being discussed, with more guidelines to come in the next few months. Some schools reopened, and the young were finally eligible for the vaccines. Cartoons popped up and jingles, too, encouraging youngsters to brave it and take the vaccines.

The guilty verdict finally came in on the case that riled up the country to expose the abysmal levels of injustice permeating the nation. The crowd outside the courthouse shouted with relief, a rarity when it comes to such a verdict in this country. The guilty officer now convicted of murder did not wear a confident smirk as he did while he deliberately choked out the life of the victim. Instead, there was some confusion in his furrowed brow, unable to process the news as quickly as the crowd outside, filled with those who were forced too many times to process injustices on a daily basis. Maybe he expected a free and clear verdict and was having issues processing real justice. He, too, would have a long day of reckoning. The family gave a press release along with their attorney, and several family members graced the podium to express heartbreak and memories of a family member taken violently too soon. This verdict was rare and a surprise for those who expected the boot of injustice yet again. It was a rare stab at accountability bringing hope to some that maybe justice was sometimes attainable.

At times, these dreams seem so real. I should remember to write them all down, but I forget. There was a long line of men, women, and children amid bombed-out rubble waiting for the foreign medical teams to help. Food came eventually, all of this during a holy turf war and what was labeled as another pandemic, with no lasting agreement in sight. There was no smoke, but a lingering thick metallic scent covered the area. This was a temporary ceasefire, lasting only for about a week. Food and medical assistance could be brought in to the citizens who did not flee. One group was solely concerned about their right to freedom, land, and opportunity, while the other side gobbled up more land and rested on the security of foreign military aid, ancient religious texts, and global support. Someone in the distance was praying aloud about a temple in dispute, then there was silence.

The blast of a horn cut through the silence, and a voice could be heard reminding a bewildered crowd that one brother would overthrow the other in the end. After decades of unrest, staggering military might, and an unquenchable thirst for more territory, the seemingly weaker brother did indeed win in the end. It was written, and so it became. There was a map in the distance of a once Great Conqueror, a former empire, where the sun supposedly never set, with all its former colonies spread across the globe, now diminished. All that was left on the map was a small mass. The crowds in the distance were no more; the rubble would not be restored.

CHAPTER 31

I hauled five bags of groceries up the stairs, plopped them down at Sean's door and rang the bell before heading back to my car, puffing down the walkway. Maybe he'll be able to get out of bed to get them before dark. I wished I could see him and say hello but couldn't risk getting sick, I had no health insurance. These impromptu quarantine sessions isolated people, and somewhat gratefully, I came to appreciate it; solace was golden.

Now, I had my own bags to unpack, disinfect and store. There was enough food for the next three weeks if I didn't eat too much. The large, orange container of disinfectant wipes sat on the kitchen counter as I walked in, my reminder to wipe everything down. Maybe it was overkill to wipe all the cartons and cans, but I got into the habit for over six months and could not break it. The disinfectant manufacturers were happy, at least some people were pleased with the results of this plague.

I reached for the buzzing phone on my hip while holding a box of cereal in my other hand.

Good, he got them.

"Thank you so much, Ms. Delivery lady! I'll deal with them later; they're at least on my kitchen counter." Sean sounded muffled. I tapped impatiently to turn on the speaker, the volume up.

"How are you feeling?" It had been five days since his positive test, and his symptoms were severe, most likely from the new strain swiftly crisscrossing the country.

"Gurl, like I got hit by a category 5. A constant headache and sweating like a pig, can hardly walk, just weak." Sean sounded congested and out of breath.

"Do you need to go to the hospital? You don't sound good." I was worried.

"That hospital is gonna kill me for sure. I'll sleep in the chair fully clothed, just in case."

"Man, these nurses won't have a problem stripping you naked when you get there. Do you have a fever?"

He chuckled, clearing his throat. "Temp was around 101 this afternoon, I'll be OK."

"Did you eat anything?"

"I'll drink the rest of my soup, can't taste nothin' anyways."

"Did you get all your shots?"

"I took one."

"Well, there is a second one, you know, you're way behind schedule." I chided him, waiting for a smart comeback.

"Look, these shots ain't working."

"Sean, they are keeping many people out of the hospital. Your symptoms could have been milder. You sound like a gummed-up freight train."

"I don't believe that."

"Why?"

"They're not even releasing the latest stats anymore, and even with all those shots, they're steadily getting new strains. Well, I'm getting my own damn antibodies now, jab free this time. Honey, I don't want these case trackers calling me asking about symptoms and quarantining. I hear that's what they do."

"OK. You need to get some rest." I could not listen to another lecture. He was probably up to his neck in podcasts with all his spare time. Was it a case of vaccine fatigue, or maybe the Q conspiracy plague was infiltrating his news feeds.

"I'll check on you in the morning. Call me if you need anything, OK."

"I'll be fine. Appreciate the groceries. Don't tell my sister about this if you talk to her."

"Bye. Get some rest."

If I talked to her, I was going to tell. Sean was not taking this seriously, plus he had a history of asthma and sometimes did not keep up with his inhaler. Too many people were checking out, dying without warning. Last week, three family members in the neighborhood died within two weeks. The youngest member only had symptoms for two days before she was admitted to the ER and died the same day. And people continued to turn up their noses at the shot. I heard about a family of eight last year who died in another state. That was in the beginning before the vaccination was rolled out.

Sean conveniently forgot that he went to the pharmacy last month but did not have the patience to wait his turn to get the second shot. Brain fog, maybe. *Doubt he'd be this sick now, but as my grandma used to say, "who can't hear gon' feel."* I had one bag of groceries left to disinfect before hitting the bed.

CHAPTER 32

I rolled over, grabbed the phone and swiped but didn't get the call in time. Squinting incredulously at my phone, it registered 12:20 AM. That was Sean, he must not be doing well, and his symptoms must have gotten worse, but I knew that the hospital was the last place he wanted to be. I listened to his message and immediately dialed the nearest hospital, frantically hoping for a response. Seven rings, eight, I hung up, redialed again, still no success. My only option now was to call his sister. As a nurse, she may be on her shift, I hoped she would answer.

"Hello…"

"Lela, your brother just called, he's not doing well. I spoke to him earlier today. He refused to go to the hospital. He does not want me to tell you. He's getting worse, you might be able to convince him."

"Oh, he has it?"

"Yes," I mumbled nervously, awaiting an outburst.

"And I spoke to him yesterday. He said nothing!" she groaned.

"Had it for several days. I missed the call. Just now, he left a message saying he has problems breathing, even sitting up in the recliner. No answer at the hospital."

"Wish I knew before I got off my shift. We have no beds, none. I don't care if he wants to go or not; he has to. Let me call

Green Medical across town and see, but I doubt they'll have room."

"OK, and I'll call the county one, just in case."

I felt helpless, knowing there was little to no room anywhere. There was no end in sight, and staffing was limited as nurses left this area for the opportunity to earn more pay traveling to other states. Everyone was tired. Was a steep climb in infections within the last two weeks, the number had tripled, and now the national guard was being deployed to help the understaffed, overworked hospital staff nationwide.

"Well, when were you going to tell me? I could kill him, spoiled brat, baby syndrome. He always got away with everything. Still being defiant, including killing himself!"

She hung up, her voice quivering. I was too rattled to even respond in time. I immediately dialed the county hospital.

After four rings, someone picked up, I couldn't believe it.

"Hello. Do you have any beds?"

"No beds available; try Bluefield; they had a few. I'm sorry ma'am." The young lady replied, probably for the fortieth time tonight.

"How far away is it?"

"At this time of night it should be less than an hour with little traffic. Right over the state line, in Pike County."

"Thank you so much." I could hear another phone ringing continuously as I hung up. Lela called back. She had exhausted her search.

"Bluefield is your only option," I shouted into the phone. She dialed Sean, hoping to add him to our conversation.

They shouted at each other, his voice raspy, as he paused every few seconds to catch a breath.

"So, who forced you all to call me at this time of the night? I didn't ask for a nurse," he snapped.

I listened to the banter but kept silent, holding in my anger.

I really shouldn't be in the middle of this nonsense past midnight, really. If you don't mind dying, I can't change that.

"Can you get your big butt to the front door? They'll be there soon." Lela shouted.

"What? Whyyy in the…?"

I was not going to be a part of this and hung up mid-sentence without a word and sent a text to Lela confirming the location.

"Bluefield. The wait should not be long, even if they run out of beds. The medics will have to deal with his attitude."

Man, I need some sleep.

"Thank you so much! On our way, Will keep you posted."

Finally, silence. Peace. I laid back, sinking into the pillows. The poor overworked nurses would have to find a way to silence him if he made it to them in time.

CHAPTER 33

The arrests came slowly, after much investigation, and the numbers were in the hundreds. The rioters were being flushed out; some a part of organized groups, and others were grumpy citizens who felt it was their duty to travel to the capital and show blind solidarity. There was a supporter in a battered costume who had previously been arrested and sentenced. Somehow, he seemed to find his theatric, suited self back into the news cycle many times since. It was reported that he wanted a softer landing in prison and was not pleased with his living arrangements. According to his attorneys, his current conditions were too harsh and were affecting his mental state. No one, however, seemed to question his mental state while he was monkeying around with his furry friends inside the chambers months ago.

Also streaming was reports of another mass shooting at another crowd-filled musical gathering. Any break in the viral onslaught was cause for celebration, and they came in droves for a concert of some sort. Mass shootings no longer gripped national attention as before. The gun lobbyist, so far, stayed ahead of the outcries that had become almost commonplace. A documentary surfaced of a mass shooting at a large venue, where security failed through lack of planning and cowardice to prevent some of the casualties. Apparently, a well-to-do shark got tired of living and losing and decided to end his life, offering up some bulleted revenge on his way out. He decided one evening to target practice with several of his extensive rifle collection pieces. Dozens lost their lives that day. Despite complaints, the routine shootings continued to escalate.

By the end of the year, the cash-stuffed venue clan kissed the local mayor on his sweaty forehead, for it was hot out there. A multitude of obligations forced him to kiss them back on their behinds, and they all seemed to have gotten off without a scratch. The grieving families settled for a pittance; no substantive memorials were ever erected for the dead as promised, and all was glitzy again. It was as if this tragedy had never happened in that city, and more profits flowed in than before the plague.

Meanwhile, there was a shortage of masks again but toilet paper was stocked piled high. The prices were triple what they were one month ago, and I loved the disposable ones. Guess I'd have to use my regulars, I hated to hand wash them every night, but at least I had some of those. The beaded ones were the worst. I had to soak and squeeze but couldn't wash them as thoroughly as the plain ones for fear of the beads falling off. There were masks for every occasion, a far cry from the onset of the virus when they were handmade from socks and scarves. Still loved my sock ones; they were very comfortable and did not cut off my ears. There were the "Hi" smiley face masks, the "Love" masks, as well as the "FU" and "Screw U" masks. There were also socially responsible masks "Justice," "Voting Rights," "Parent Rights," "My Rights" and there were the "Poor Me," and "Why Me," the complaining ones.

CHAPTER 34

Family and friends arrived about half an hour earlier to take their assigned seats before the dinner and memorial event. The hall was large, decorated in a black and white theme with navy blue centerpieces. Navy was coincidentally the favorite color of both members being remembered tonight. There was a banner on the wall behind the podium, and both large screens on the side walls offered collages of graduations past, family photos, and highlights of life events and accolades. Somber music could be heard in the background as friends and neighbors mingled, slowly finding their way to the round tables that were arranged throughout the large hall.

Melva hoped there would be enough room, as the group anticipated a great turnout for this cause. Her husband B and a few neighbors sat on the left, close to the podium, with her die-hard group of friends. I sat in silence and looked at the somber faces of the family members who were still grieving the loss. Another part of the group staked claim to their chairs nearby as the event was about to begin. It was 7 p.m., and dinner would be served momentarily. The caterers were ready to serve the meal and, thankfully, offered to volunteer their services for the evening. A group of five, these ladies took care of every detail as they did for every fundraising event they were entrusted to. The memorial guests tonight would be served with real dinnerware donated by a local restaurant and include a choice of four desserts.

B surveyed the menu options with a grin, pulling his reading glasses down, hoping to calm his wife. "What's on this menu tonight? Smashed, hmm, sauteed, steamed and un-steamed?" The servers were taking orders, and a decision had to be made.

"We've got top notch catering tonight," Melva commented loudly.

"Well, I could try the eggplant?" B mumbled. She looked over at him, shocked.

"It's all vegetarian, you know. No meat stuffed inside like you think."

"Oh? Never mind, I'll pass. What are you having?"

"Chicken is always good. I've got to get all the names correctly before I get up there." She was preoccupied as the waiter took the orders as she readied herself to give the much-anticipated speech. As the guests enjoyed the meal, she slowly headed toward the podium stopping to chat at a few tables nearby. The opening was brief, given by an elder in the community. He was followed by family members offering their memories and reflections on the lives of their loved ones lost too soon during the last few months. A young lady recited a long poem about life after loss, as the live band resumed, and the guests enjoyed dessert.

The ticket price was a bit steep for the average neighbor, but it was decided by the Sisters on the Pulse that as a fundraiser for both families, it would be worth the cost. There was half an hour of additional entertainment provided by students from the nearby high school. There were already rave reviews that the meal was outstanding. So far, they were delivering. It was a slam dunk, sold out due to online advertising and word of mouth. A lively flute performance was coming to an end as Melva walked toward the podium. Many wiped away tears as images flashed on the screen of the vibrant lives they had lived.

"Ladies and gentlemen, thank you for your presence and generosity as we gather to celebrate the lives of Paula and Ricky," Melva continued. "Let's be honest; it has been a hell of a year." She paused until the resounding applause and shouts from the guests died down. The tribute was long, the room silent, as she offered comfort to the families before a solemn conclusion.

"Let us remember the precious time and the memories we were privileged to be a part of while they were with us. They were taken in their prime, like so many during this pandemic. They are gone too soon. We do not know what the future will bring, how many more strains are to come, how many future disasters and how many more lives will be lost. While we are here, let us live each day to the fullest, drawing strength from our creator, remembering each day, who and what's most important in our lives, and continue to support each other and our communities at this time."

There were tears, as there had been before; the night ended with rousing applause followed by an interpretive dance troupe performance and a floral presentation to both families. The mood was somber. The crowd thinned out somewhat quickly as guests exited the amiable comfort of the room into the blustery night, readying for another tomorrow, a Monday of uncertainty and trepidation.

EPILOGUE

B has always made time for the 6:00 p.m. news. Before he retired, if he had no overtime scheduled, he would come home, pull off his cap and drop into his favorite recliner in the corner and flip on the news. With much more free time he has added the midday news to his lineup and some nights the 11pm roundup. He chooses the stations that keep him abreast of global news and never tires of the realities around him, grim as they may be. He understands hunger and national instability firsthand. As a boy, he remembers people not having enough to eat, national worker strikes, the burning of fields of harvest and the struggle for basic human dignity. B keeps abreast of the newest strains of the virus and the disturbing daily news stories. He reminds Melva that there is no proof any vaccinations can offer a solution to the onslaught of present and future outbreaks and that many more will continue to die. He is aware of a curious new viral too, a pox, and reminds her of the symptoms that the infected will experience - like painful bumps flaring in obscure and delicate places of the nether regions that will, in time, leave lots of scarring. Melva tells him every day to stop telling her more bad news so she could save her energies for community outreach. The fires will continue to increase, and the hurricanes across the globe too, he warns her.

Like so many during this crisis, life has taken an uncertain turn. I will embrace the newfound freedom and wide path ahead, unclear as it may be. The boys were back to school full-time, and I am relieved that Luanne has lined up another assistant on an as-needed basis. My friend who worked with Luanne before has declined the offer to go back to work with the family. Melva recently asked me to assist as a coordinator for a senior project she recently spearheaded with several other community organizers. She needed 'warm bodies' as 'Lifelines for Seniors,' the name of the project, who can reach out to offer education, support, access to care and community. The most exciting addition to the project is to offer reliable transportation to assist with errands and to and from medical appointments. Many retirees in the community are unaware or unable to access these resources, and the outreach has begun. I am grateful to be a part of this much-needed service and have offered three days a week to the project.

We lost a great woman, Ms. Pauletta, a stellar example for future generations. She died four months after her dear boyfriend Vernon. They both passed away at the senior living facility. I wished I could have combed her hair one more time as she begged me to during our last virtual meeting. She lost her spunk after he died and wore black every day, she told me, even donning a matching head tie. Her funeral was filled with neighbors, friends far and wide and even a few dignitaries. She did not know how great her impact was, her words of wisdom, her great stories of encouragement, and the giving of her time. She financially supported several children, three of whom came forward to tell their stories for the first time. Even on a limited budget, she extended a helping hand to those in need for many years. One of the children she discreetly supported was now a local superintendent of schools. Written on the cover of her funeral program were these words, her mantra. "Don't worry, every little bit helps. It's all the Lord's work."

Sean is now on a weight loss journey. He survived the ordeal and learned that hospitals could be useful institutions, sometimes. He walks four days a week, through the neighborhood, with a towel on his shoulder and begged me not to laugh at his huffing. I do not. I admire his will to change and his tenacity despite his lingering respiratory issues. He seems more relaxed and grateful and is overall in a better place with his family and his mood is ten times calmer.

Will finally has his original employees back to their regular schedules, except one, and has had to hire three more part-time workers because business is booming. Despite the rumblings of people moving away from the bustle to safer and less expensive areas of the state, the restaurant is at capacity on most nights, and on the weekend, the wait is long. He lost one of his cooks to the virus and now has a memorial in his honor at the entrance to the restaurant. As before, he treats the ladies to their favorite drinks at their long reserved table, usually once a week. The prospect of opening another restaurant is in the works. He keeps the details close to his vest and has the perfect location in mind. Everyone is still recovering, there may be another outbreak, and he thinks it's best to wait a few months just to be safe.

Melva and the Ladies on the Pulse, along with concerned citizens everywhere, will continue their weekly meetings, ruminating on ideas and policies to affect change, protect what is thriving and blaze new trails. The weekly threats will not stop any of them; they sure will not stop me. Life will continue as it has from the bosom of creation to be precious. In due time, persons and countries who choose to dictate whose life is dear and who is not, those who demean, discard, and dispose of life at will, shall have a seismic reckoning. Those who respect living and loving will continue to thrive and explore life intricacies and will find fulfillment and purpose.

Mrs. V knows the ins and outs of living, she has done so for over seven decades, and it shows in her deep furrows, fine lines in her cheeks and her thin silver cornrows. She almost lost a nephew from the virus recently and was saddened that he did not reveal his illness to the family until it was almost too late. Now he is having respiratory issues and some mental health challenges that require daily care. Since he cannot work and is unable to fend for himself at this time, she helps to take care of him and vows to do so for as long as she can. She has given up childcare for the moment to focus on her nephew. For generations, she has been a fighter. Like she told me, 'this here is no big deal,' she has wrestled with 'trifling floozies,' found herself, outlived a 'decent cheatin' man' and is still here.

ABOUT THE AUTHOR

Serene T. Marshall was born on the island of Grenada, where she spent her formative years, and now lives on the Mississippi Gulf Coast. She has earned degrees in literature from Colgate University and the University of North Carolina at Charlotte. Serene's articles have appeared in the *Boston Globe* and the *Charlotte Observer*.

If you enjoyed this book, please take time to leave a review.